She wasn't too surprised by the light grip on her arm that followed, having half expected a man like Adam was proving to be wouldn't just meekly accept *being* dismissed. But she intended keeping this as brief as possible.

The warmth in his dark brown eyes as she turned back to face him unnerved her a little, though. And he made no effort to remove the warmth of his hand from her arm, either—long, tapered fingers very deeply tanned against her much paler skin.

'You really shouldn't marry that guy, you know.' His voice was huskily intimate, giving the impression that they were the only two people in the room.

Another book you will enjoy
by CAROLE MORTIMER

THE LOVING GIFT

Just because David Kendrick fell in love with
Jade at first sight, it didn't mean she had to put
up with his impulsive pursuit of her. He might be
handsome and charming, but she had a past
from which she was still running, and which
would one day come between them. So it was
better, wasn't it, not to start anything?

ELUSIVE AS
THE UNICORN

BY

CAROLE MORTIMER

MILLS & BOON LIMITED
ETON HOUSE   18-24 PARADISE ROAD
RICHMOND   SURREY   TW9 1SR

*First published in Great Britain 1989
by Mills & Boon Limited*

© Carole Mortimer 1989

*Australian copyright 1989
Philippine copyright 1989
This edition 1989*

ISBN 0 263 76346 3

*Set in Times Roman 11 on 12¼ pt.
01-8907-43314 C*

Made and printed in Great Britain

For
Matthew and Joshua

CHAPTER ONE

'WHY did you let him do that to you?'

The smile that had curved Eve's lips faded, as she turned to face the owner of that intrusive voice, and was replaced by a puzzled frown. She didn't know the man who stood in front of her; in fact, she was sure she had never even seen him before, for she would never have forgotten such ruggedly perfect features on any man. He didn't have that pretty-pretty type of male looks that such a lot of women seemed to find so attractive nowadays, but a craggily stamped handsomeness that even her male-critical grandmother would have acknowledged as being 'all man'. But still, Eve was sure she had never seen him before.

'I'm sorry?' She looked at him enquiringly.

Dark brown eyes snapped with impatience as the man towered over her diminutive five feet two inches in height in her three-inch-high sandals, the man's dark blond hair brushing the collar of his white evening shirt. 'Why the hell did you take such a load of chauvinistic bull from the guy who just left you?' he demanded disgustedly, shaking his head, as if her behaviour utterly amazed him.

Eve gave an exasperated smile; after all, who was this man, to have been eavesdropping on her con-

versation with Paul in the first place? The fact that
he was an American in no way excused his incredible rudeness in talking to her in this way, even
if this was a party.

'I'm sorry, Mr...?' She paused deliberately,
giving him the opportunity to introduce himself to
her at least.

An opportunity he didn't feel it necessary to take.
'So you keep saying,' he rasped in that husky drawl
that had annoyed her the first time she'd heard it—
and done little to endear itself to her since! 'But
it's time someone told you that you can't go through
life apologising for being alive.'

Enough was enough, even from a man who obviously had no idea how offensive he was being,
his dark gaze raking over her with impatient
demand. 'Obviously no one could ever accuse you
of that.' Sarcasm dripped icily off her voice, her
expression one of haughty disdain—her 'Little Miss
Aloof look', as her grandmother called it.

Humour lightened the darkness of the man's
gaze. 'You can bet your sweet—— No, no one ever
has yet,' he amended mockingly, making no
apology for the language he had been about to use.
'And I don't intend they ever should, either!' he
added grimly.

Eve gave a quizzical smile. This really was too
ridiculous, a man she had never seen before ver-
bally attacking her in this way, and so personally
too. 'I'll bear your advice in mind, Mr...?'

'You'll have to do more than that if you intend seeing that guy again.' He sipped the alcohol—probably whisky—from the glass in his hand, glancing across the room to where Paul now stood engaged in conversation with a group of other guests, again making no effort to take up her very obvious opening for him to introduce himself. 'At the moment you're nothing more than a walking doormat!'

This conversation had been far from amusing from the first; now it was positively insulting! 'Since I didn't ask for your advice—or your opinion—I'll thank you to keep them both to yourself.' Blue eyes flashed her irritation.

The man grinned, a hugely appreciative grin. 'I see the mouse can roar if she wants to,' he drawled derisively, his gaze openly challenging.

'This *mouse* happens to be going to marry the "guy" across the room!' she informed him caustically.

She stood stiffly, deeply resentful of his personal remarks about Paul and herself. How on earth had he got an invitation to one of Lady Daphne Graves's parties? Heaven knew, Daphne was far from being a snob, but Eve just couldn't believe the other woman would have given an invitation to such a socially destructive man.

His grin had faded the moment she made her announcement. 'You're *marrying* him?' He gave a pained wince at the idea. 'Why?' His eyes narrowed.

Eve's own triumphant smile at having momentarily disconcerted him instantly disappeared at his bluntly put question. 'Why?' she echoed exasperatedly. 'You ask the strangest questions.' She shook her head. 'Questions that obviously need no answer.'

'This one sure does,' the man scorned. 'Why would you want to tie yourself for life to a man who orders you to wait for him here—and obviously expects you to obey him without question—while he circulates among the other guests, enjoying himself?'

'Paul didn't *order* me to stay here!' Eve's cheeks were flushed with indignant anger.

'No?' the man beside her derided scoffingly. 'It sounded like it to me.'

'It wasn't like that at all,' she denied defensively. 'He simply asked me to wait for him here while he——'

'Circulated.' The man's opinion of that was obvious from his tone.

'It's important that Paul meet people like this,' Eve told him in annoyance, inwardly wondering why she was even bothering to explain herself; her relationship with Paul was none of this man's business. 'He makes vital contacts at parties like this one.'

Dark brown eyes levelled derisively on Paul as he continued his conversation across the room. 'I'm sure he does,' the man said with obvious distaste. 'But those contacts might be a little more impressed with *him* if he paid more attention to the woman he intends to marry!'

Paul had turned to look at them curiously now, a question in his light blue eyes as his gaze met Eve's, a question Eve didn't have the answer to; she didn't even have the benefit of knowing this man's name, let alone why he should have chosen to single her out for his insulting remarks!

He shook his head now, blonder highlights picked out in the dark blond hair by the illuminated crystal chandelier above them. 'Most of the women I know would have told that guy to take a hike if he had ordered them to stay put,' he remarked, implying she should have done the same if she'd had any sense.

Eve held herself stiffly erect at his insistence that Paul had 'ordered' her to do anything. 'I don't believe we've been introduced yet?' she prompted resentfully, her mouth set in an angry line.

He gave a mocking smile. 'I'm not allowed to insult you until you know my name, hm?' he taunted in that slow drawl.

She gave an impatient sigh. 'I just thought it might be more—polite.' She couldn't help wishing that Paul would stop just looking at them with narrowed eyes, and actually come over here and rescue her from this unpleasant conversation.

The man at her side gave a dismissive shrug as she looked at him with steady query. 'Most people call me Adam. Although I'm sure it isn't the only name I've ever been known as,' he added with a humorous glint in his eyes.

She could imagine it wasn't the only name he had ever been called to his face, either; men who could be as personal as this one was, without even the benefit of a proper introduction, must get used to being told a few home truths about themselves!

However, the single name he had given her was enough to make Eve give an inward groan. 'Well, Adam——'

'Isn't it usual to reciprocate?' Chocolate-coloured eyes openly laughed at her for her deliberate omission, as if he were already in on the joke of their names, although she felt sure he couldn't be.

Her inward groan became a cry for help; considering how brutally frank he had been about something that was none of his business, she hated to think what comment he was going to make about their two names—Adam and Eve!

Nothing like this had ever happened to her before. Oh, during her childhood her friends had done the usual teasing about her name, and how she was 'waiting for her Adam', but the man's name hadn't been one that was popular at the time of her birth or for several years before that, and so, strange as it might seem, men named Adam had been distinctly missing from her life. Until now.

Why on earth did this man, a man who already found her such a source of amusement and a recipient of his pity, have to be called Adam?

'Eve,' she muttered with all the heartfelt reluctance she knew.

Dark blond brows quirked over questioning eyes as he leant down towards her slightly. 'I'm sorry, I didn't quite catch that.'

She gave an impatient sigh. 'I really shouldn't keep you from your companion for the evening any longer,' she dismissed with light finality.

'I came with a couple of friends,' he shrugged, equally dismissively.

Eve's interest flickered into life in spite of herself; somehow she had half expected him to be in the company of one of the svelte model-types here that would probably be more to his liking than the tiny blonde that she was, her slender figure complemented by the petrol-blue dress she wore rather than the other way around, her shoulder-length hair framing a heart-shaped face that was dominated by dark-lashed blue eyes. And while half of her had believed this man would be accompanied by a woman who was the complete opposite of herself, the other half of her had queried what he was doing talking to *her* if he had come with a fascinating woman like that? But he had said a couple of friends...

'A married couple,' Adam supplied in a mocking tone, as if he had guessed the direction of her thoughts—as he probably had! 'They aren't going to be in the least concerned by my disappearance; they know I'm here to meet someone.'

Her eyes widened, large blue pools lightened almost to turquoise by naturally thick, dark lashes. 'I don't think Daphne throws those sort of parties,' she derided.

'Someone special,' he added softly.

Her brows quirked. 'Even so...'

'Someone *very* special,' he mocked.

He sounded so positive, as if he had someone definite in mind. Or as if, once he had found the woman he was interested in, he would have no trouble whatsoever in convincing her she was interested in him too! And, probably, he usually didn't.

'Then I hope you succeed in meeting her,' Eve told him briskly, ash-blonde hair moving silkily about her shoulders as she straightened dismissively.

'Daphne doesn't throw *those* sort of parties,' he reminded drily.

A delicate blush brightened her cheeks. '*I* know that,' she said sharply, wishing once again that Paul would forget those 'vital contacts to his career' for once and rejoin her.

He was deep in conversation with Lord Graves at the moment, although to give him his due she could see Lord Graves was doing most of the talking, Paul's attention distracted, as his mind was half on the fact that a complete stranger had engaged Eve in conversation for the last ten minutes or so.

'So do I,' Adam derided softly. 'I'm here to meet a legend.'

Eve gave a puzzled frown at the announcement. There were some very important and internationally renowned people here tonight, titled people, politicians, others from the world of theatre and music, all of them mingling as equals, specifically invited for their ability to make this yet another social triumph for Lady Daphne; it wouldn't *be* a Lady Daphne party if it weren't a social success. But, as far as Eve was aware, famous as some of these people were, or were going to be, none of them merited being called a legend. Not yet, anyway!

'Are you sure you have the right party?' she taunted wryly.

Some of the confidence left him as he too glanced around the elegantly furnished drawing-room of the Graveses' at the assortment of people gathered there. 'I hope so,' he finally frowned. 'Sophy assured me——'

'Sophy?' Eve echoed sharply, shooting Paul a worried glance, relieved to see he still couldn't escape Dudley Graves, a complete contradiction of her thoughts of a few moments ago. Her gaze returned to Adam. 'Do you mean Sophy O'Donnell?' she put the question casually.

He nodded, a frown still marring his perfectly sculpted brow. 'She and her husband are the couple that brought me here tonight.'

She had already guessed as much, just as she could now realise to which 'legend' he referred. Paul

wasn't going to like it one little bit when he found
out what Sophy had been up to.

Not that it was too difficult to work out the
reason for the other woman's bloody-mindedness;
she hadn't liked it one bit when Paul had proved
difficult about the 'showing' at her gallery this
winter, and had obviously decided to be a little
awkward herself by bringing this man Adam to this
party, a man intent on meeting a 'legend', even if
that legend didn't want to be met—or recognised.

Sophy and Patrick O'Donnell owned and ran one
of the most prestigious art galleries in London;
Sophy was a shrewd businesswoman who hated to
be told no, and let no one forget it. Even a 'legend'
who she knew chose to remain anonymous.

Eve fixed a bright smile on her pastel-pink
painted lips. 'Then I really shouldn't keep you any
longer. I have to go and talk to Paul anyway,' she
added quickly, as it seemed Adam might begin to
protest.

The mockery returned to dark brown eyes.
'That's allowed, is it?'

Her mouth tightened, but she forced the smile to
remain on her lips; she wanted to get away from
him, and *stay* away from him, and engaging in
another verbal exchange with him wouldn't achieve
that. 'I hope you enjoy the rest of the party, Adam.'
She nodded dismissively before turning away.

She wasn't too surprised by the light grip on her
arm that followed, having half expected a man like
Adam was proving to be wouldn't just meekly

accept *being* dismissed. But she intended keeping this as brief as possible.

The warmth in his dark brown eyes as she turned back to face him unnerved her a little, though. And he made no effort to remove the warmth of his hand from her arm, either—long, tapered fingers very deeply tanned against her much paler skin.

'You really shouldn't marry that guy, you know.' His voice was huskily intimate, giving the impression that they were the only two people in the room.

Irritation snapped in her eyes. She had waited a long time for Paul to notice her, and now that he had she wasn't about to listen to the uninformed opinion of a complete stranger concerning the two of them. What did this man *really* know about them?

'You'll bear my advice in mind, right?' he derided with a shake of his head. 'But it's more than advice, Miss Whoever-you-are,' he added with serious intent, his eyes narrowed. 'If you marry Paul with your relationship the way it is, then the marriage— or you—is doomed for disaster, depending which breaks down first.'

Eve felt a shiver of apprehension down her spine, and then instantly dismissed it. She had known and loved Paul most of her life; what could this man, who didn't know Paul at all, possibly know of that love? He certainly had no right to pass an opinion on it on such short acquaintance!

'Paul and I will be very happy together,' she told the man at her side stiffly.

His mouth twisted. 'Is that what he told you?' he countered.

She drew in an indignant breath. 'You really are the most arrogant——' She broke off, stunned at her own vehemence, her cheeks fiery red. 'What I meant to say was——'

'You were doing just fine before,' he mocked her distress. 'Talk to your Paul a few times like that, and I doubt he would order you to stay put for too much longer.'

'He didn't—— Oh, really, Adam, I don't think there's any point in continuing this conversation.' She shook off his hand impatiently, slightly disturbed when she could still feel the warm imprint of it against her skin. 'You simply don't understand my relationship with Paul.' And you never will, her tone implied.

How could he possibly understand a love like the one she had for Paul, and Paul had for her? Adam himself seemed to be free of such emotion, and probably always had been.

'I understand love,' he told her softly. 'I've witnessed the genuine article between my own parents for the last thirty-eight years.' And what you have with Paul isn't it, *his* tone seemed to imply.

'You——'

'Sorry to have left you so long, darling,' interrupted a dearly familiar voice, Paul's arm moving lightly about her waist as he came to stand beside her. 'But you seem to have been kept amused.' He looked enquiringly at the other man.

Eve turned to him gladly, feeling her heart skip its usual beat as she gazed up into his handsome face.

A little under six feet in height, Paul was possessed of a natural male elegance, had naturally wavy dark hair that was styled just long enough for that natural wave to be apparent, dark lashes surrounding eyes that were that curious colour that was neither blue nor grey, but could be both, or somewhere in between.

At thirty, just four years older than Eve herself, Paul was nevertheless able to meet the older man's assessing gaze with equal confidence. And why shouldn't he? No matter who this man Adam turned out to be—and he had to be *someone* for Sophy to have bothered with him!—Paul was a successful man in his own right.

'I hope she has,' the man called Adam replied. 'You really shouldn't leave this lovely lady alone for too long.'

Eve could feel the resentment in Paul at the casually made remark as he stiffened at her side. And with just cause!

She shot the man called Adam a quelling glance, frowning her impatience as he blandly returned her gaze with feigned innocence.

'Eve is perfectly able to—— What on earth!' Paul said in an astounded voice as the other man began to chuckle at his remark.

Eve understood Adam's humour only too well, giving a pained wince as the chuckle became a full-throated laugh, causing more than a few people to look their way. Adam's eyes were full of merriment as he chokingly excused himself when he couldn't contain the humour, crossing the room to enter the garden through the open patio doors. The sound of his laughter could still be heard coming from outside, causing even more curious looks to be directed at Eve and Paul.

Eve's face was bright red with embarrassment as Paul looked down at her with angry eyes; he hated having any unnecessary attention drawn to him.

But she couldn't be held responsible for Adam's spontaneous humour—at least, not through any deliberate intent on her part. And she very much doubted that Paul would appreciate the 'Adam and Eve' significance that had been the cause of the other man's uncontrollable laughter.

'What was all that about?' Paul demanded through gritted teeth, the forced smile to his lips trying to claim that he saw nothing unusual in someone going off into peals of laughter after being spoken to!

She shook her head. 'I think he must have had a little too much to drink.' She tried to shrug off the embarrassing episode.

Paul gazed after the other man, his frown lightening slightly. 'Perhaps,' he murmured thoughtfully. 'Yes, you're probably right,' he decided with brisk dismissal, turning back to her. 'Who was he, anyway?' he said irritably.

She shrugged, keeping her tone light. 'I have no idea.'

The heavy frown returned. 'You weren't introduced?'

'No,' she admitted tightly, reluctantly. 'And he didn't chose to introduce himself either,' she dismissed.

The name Adam couldn't really be classed as an introduction, and the little else she did know about him—that Sophy O'Donnell had brought him here to meet a 'legend'—wasn't guaranteed to endear him to Paul. In fact, the opposite was true. Sophy was one of the least popular people with Paul at the moment.

'Damned cheek of the man.' He glared at the open french doors with narrowed eyes. 'What did he want?' His gaze returned assessingly to Eve.

Mainly to dissuade her from marrying Paul! And that conversation was laughable now; now that she was with Paul, that brief shiver of apprehension she had felt earlier was completely forgotten. 'Nothing, really,' she dismissed brightly, a glowing smile on her lips as she looked lovingly into Paul's face. 'I think he was just at a loose end, having come with a married couple.' She deliberately omitted to mention *which* married couple it had been. 'I can't even remember what we talked about now,' she assured.

Paul still looked stern. 'You really shouldn't engage in conversation with complete strangers,

Eve.' He shook his head reprovingly. 'I've told you before, you're too trusting.'

'Darling,' she placated tenderly, her hand resting lightly on his arm, 'it was only small talk. And he did realise I was here with you,' she reminded teasingly, pushing firmly from her mind the other man's disparaging remarks. 'Now, why don't we start to enjoy this party?'

Together. The word popped into her mind without volition, and she frowned her irritation at letting the man Adam's comments affect her enough to allow even one detrimental thought about Paul to disturb her in this way. Paul had his career to think about and, although she wasn't really into parties herself, she respected the fact that functions like this were important to him. The man Adam just didn't understand that, didn't understand the nature of their relationship.

Paul dismissed the other man with effort, and they did begin to circulate together among the other guests.

But two of the people she and Paul did avoid during the next hour, as they moved among the chattering groups about the room, were Sophy and Patrick O'Donnell. If Paul saw the two couples were about to meet, then he neatly avoided it without being too obvious. And that suited Eve too, mainly because the man Adam was with the other couple for the majority of the evening, a fact Paul didn't seem to have realised. Thank goodness!

But Sophy wasn't about to take that sort of treatment all evening; she was much more force-fully direct than her amiably friendly husband, and Eve wasn't at all surprised to see the beautiful redhead determinedly crossing the room towards them after an hour of being avoided in that way, Patrick resignedly following in her wake. To Eve's relief, it was one of the occasions the man Adam had briefly wandered away from them. Probably in search of his living 'legend'!

'Eve, Paul——' She gave the latter a brittle smile, standing almost as tall as him at five feet ten inches in her high-heeled shoes, her model-thin body shown to advantage in the black glittering evening dress. 'I thought it was time we came over and said hello.' The smile she bestowed on Eve was much warmer, even the cynicism that usually hardened her green eyes lessening momentarily as she looked at her. 'Or did you intend the dodging game to con-tinue all evening?' Her eyes hardened once again as her gaze returned to Paul, her stance challenging.

Paul coldly met that gaze. 'I don't play games, Sophy,' he bit out.

'No,' her red-painted mouth tightened, 'you're too damned arrogant for that. You——'

'Darling,' Patrick stepped in with his usual easy self-control, a tall, loose-limbed man with untidy dark hair, his casual appearance hiding a very great talent. Sophy was the businesswoman in their marriage-partnership, while Patrick was the expe-rienced art dealer and collector.

On the surface they were an unlikely-looking couple—Sophy so worldly and cynical, Patrick bordering on the absent-minded genius—and yet their differing personalities complemented each other, softening Sophy's more brittle nature, while Patrick's love and admiration for his wife drew him more out into the world than he might otherwise have been.

Sophy glanced at her husband, and at his warning look she brushed off her irritation with a sigh, relaxing slightly. 'Are you both having a good time?' she enquired lightly.

'Not bad, thanks,' Paul answered for them stiltedly, completely unbending in his own resentment.

Green eyes flashed angrily. 'I gather you haven't reconsidered my suggestion about the showing at the gallery for the winter?' she snapped, completely impervious to Patrick's warning for caution now, her quick-fire temper getting the better of her in the face of Paul's bloody-mindedness.

Paul returned her gaze coldly. 'Have you?'

'Come on, you two,' Patrick interrupted lightly, shooting Eve an apologetic smile. 'This is no place to be discussing business.'

Sophy continued to glare at Paul for several tension-filled seconds before slowly relaxing, putting her arm warmly through the crook of Patrick's. 'Sorry, Eve,' she grimaced ruefully. 'I'll call you in the week, shall I, and the four of us can have dinner together one evening?'

Eve glanced up uncertainly at Paul, knowing by the remoteness of his expression that the suggestion didn't please him at all. He and Sophy just didn't get on; the other woman epitomised everything he disliked in a woman: independent even in marriage, totally self-confident in her own capabilities and, worst of all in his eyes, she was a businesswoman.

But Eve didn't have it in her to be rude to the other couple. 'That would be lovely,' she awkwardly accepted.

Sophy couldn't resist giving Paul a triumphant smile before turning away. 'I'll be in touch,' she promised before moving off, Patrick talking to her quietly as they crossed the room.

'Damned woman,' Paul muttered, not caring whether or not the other couple were out of earshot. 'I can't stand pushy women who——'

'Darling, we can't avoid seeing them forever; Sophy is right about that,' she cajoled.

His eyes narrowed with dislike. 'They aren't the only gallery in town.'

She gave him a reproving look. 'They're the best in their field,' she reminded softly.

He gave a disgruntled snort. 'We'll see.'

Eve felt an uneasy feeling in the pit of her stomach. Sophy and Patrick were highly respected in the art world—by the artists themselves, other dealers, and buyers alike—and Paul had to realise the importance, without losing any of his stiff-backed pride, of remaining politely friendly with them, even if he chose not to make them his friends.

'I have something I need to finish discussing with Dudley Graves before we leave,' he informed her abruptly, before she could voice any of her misgivings.

Eve frowned her disappointment. 'Oh, but——'

'I shouldn't be too long,' he added dismissively, before walking away without a second glance.

It was just her luck—bad luck!—that Paul should have to leave her side just at a time when the man Adam was on his own a few feet away. Her attempt to put some distance between them was thwarted as she saw-him make a determined move towards her.

'I thought he was never going to leave—Eve,' he murmured conspiratorially behind her when she hastily turned away.

Her mouth was set in disapproving lines as she turned back to face him. 'I thought your complaint was that Paul left me alone too much?' she derided drily, her brows arched mockingly.

Adam looked more rakish than ever, the gentle early summer breeze outside obviously having ruffled his dark blond hair, but only adding to his attraction in the process. 'That was my first school of thought,' he replied, coming to stand in front of her, effectively blocking out the rest of the room with his height and the width of his shoulders, shoulders that had no trouble at all filling out the jacket of the black evening suit he wore. 'We both know what my second one was,' he added taunt-ingly. 'And I haven't changed my mind about that one.'

Her impatience increased. 'You have no idea what you're talking about,' she snapped, annoyed that an evening she had thought would at least be pleasantly enjoyable had turned into a complete farce.

'OK.' He held up his hands defensively. 'Whatever you say. I don't feel like arguing with you on the subject again just now, anyway.'

She looked at him curiously. 'You aren't en-joying the party?'

'The party is just fine.' He shrugged disin-terestedly. 'As parties go,' he added in a bored voice. 'But as far as meeting The Unicorn goes, it seems to have been a waste of my time.' He sighed heavily.

The Unicorn. Eve had known the last time they spoke to which 'legend' he referred, of course, and in this case The Unicorn was an artist of ethereal beauty, who had come to the notice of the general public a little over three years ago, the paintings now collector's pieces, every one worth thousands rather than hundreds. And what added to the interest in the artist was the anonymity of the sig-nature at the bottom of all the paintings; very few people were actually in on the secret of the real identity of The Unicorn.

Obviously Adam had come to the party this evening intending to be added to their number. And

Sophy had encouraged him to believe that could happen.

'After wandering around myself for a while—which was how I first came to speak to you,' he said drily, 'I started to follow Sophy and Patrick around instead,' he muttered, obviously far from happy. 'No one they've talked to here could possibly be The Unicorn.'

Eve's brows arched at his complete certainty. 'No?'

'No.' Adam sighed, the laughter that had been so apparent in him earlier in the evening having faded as he became disillusioned as to his success in finding the person he had come here specifically to see.

'You sound very certain,' she prompted lightly, one of those privileged few who did know the identity of the artist, and their desire for privacy. She also knew that the artist *was* here at the party...

'I am.' Adam nodded firmly. 'The Unicorn is someone who sees the world with a beauty and innocence it couldn't hope to achieve; most of the people here can't see past the end of their noses!' he dismissed with unmistakable disgust.

Eve had to smile at his scorn for these people, who were, after all, just trying to enjoy themselves. 'You could be completely wrong about your artist, you know. Maybe The Unicorn is someone who paints the world the way he has cynically decided other people would like to see it, not the way he really sees it.' She couldn't resist teasing him.

He didn't look amused, more as if she had struck him. 'It couldn't be.' He shook his head disbelievingly. 'No,' he said again, as if trying to convince himself, 'I've dreamt of the moment I would meet The Unicorn...' he added flatly, his frown pained.

'You might not even like him if you met him,' she frowned, moved by the intensity of his emotion; The Unicorn's paintings obviously meant a lot to him. 'You could be disillusioned,' she said slowly. 'Disappointed.'

'I—I couldn't be.' Adam shook his head. 'Artists paint from the heart, the soul,' he insisted, the uncertainty still darkening his eyes.

She shrugged. 'Some of them just paint for the money.'

'Not The Unicorn.' He sounded more firm.

Eve could see that, although she had shaken him slightly with the things she had said, his belief in the artist was complete.

'You're right,' she told him softly. Annoying as this man had been to her all evening, she couldn't bear for the disillusionment in his eyes to continue a moment longer. 'The Unicorn doesn't paint for the money.'

His expression instantly brightened, and he moved a step closer to her. 'You know who he is!' he pounced with restrained excitement.

Eve instantly regretted her lapse, looking around the room searchingly for Paul, panic welling up inside her; he would be most displeased if he knew she had revealed even this much to a complete stranger. Especially one that had already irritated him so much!

Narrowed brown eyes moved questioningly over the pale distress of her face, Adam's head turning as he followed the direction of her frantic gaze.

His loud swallow could be clearly heard. 'Hell, no...' he groaned, as if in pain.

Eve turned back to him sharply. 'What is it?' she gasped nervously.

He had the look of someone who had just been punched in the stomach and was still reeling from the blow. 'You were right,' he said weakly. 'It would have been better if I'd never tried to find out who The Unicorn was.'

She blinked, paling even more. 'You *know* who it is?' She swallowed hard.

He nodded. 'And I've only spoken to the other man once, briefly, but I disliked him before I even met him,' he said dully.

Eve continued to look at him frowningly for several dazed seconds before his complete meaning became clear to her. And then she realised that he thought Paul was The Unicorn.

When, in actual fact, *she* was...

CHAPTER TWO

'DELICIOUSLY wicked of me, wasn't it, darling?' Sophy said with undisguised glee, her movements graceful as she strolled around Eve's studio; the mid-afternoon sunshine, as it shone through the huge window overhead, highlighting the brightness of her hair. 'I would have given anything to have seen Paul's face when he rejoined you, and Adam asked him outright if he was The Unicorn!'

Eve hadn't found it in the least amusing at the time, and she didn't particularly find it so now; Paul had made his displeasure at being taken for the artist more than plain on several occasions since the incident. However, Adam couldn't exactly be blamed for making the mistake; it had been generally accepted for some time that the artist had to be a man, and she *had* admitted to knowing the artist.

She grimaced now. 'You should have seen *Adam's* face when Paul replied, ''Good heavens, no!'' and walked off.' Dragging her along at his side!

Sophy made a face. 'The trouble with Paul is that he's a damned snob.'

Eve gave a rueful smile, having long ago given up trying to curb Sophy's acid tongue where Paul

was concerned; simply ignoring her where possible.
'He's a respectable lawyer who likes to be thought
of as such,' she corrected chidingly.

The other woman shrugged. 'As I said, he's a
damned snob. The mistake wouldn't have been
made at all if he wasn't so damned adamant about
keeping your identity a secret,' she added disgustedly, her make-up as perfect in the clear light
of day as it had been at the party two evenings ago.

Eve sighed, having heard the argument many
times before, from both sides. 'Sophy——'

'I wouldn't mind,' the other woman continued
angrily. 'But he isn't at all averse to using the money
you earn from your paintings to help further his
political ambitions.'

Sophy was the daughter of an old friend of Eve's
grandmother, and it had been through her grandmother's urgings that Eve had finally shown the
other woman some of her paintings four years ago.
Sophy, in her usual fashion, had turned out to be
abrasively honest about her work. But her criticism
of Eve's work then had been justified, and it was
because of that honesty, and the faith Sophy had
had that she could be a great artist, that she had
been able to have her first small exhibition almost
a year later.

Her criticism of Paul, Eve felt less able to accept
without demur.

'We're going to be married, Sophy,' she reminded stiffly. 'It's only natural that I should want
to help further my husband's career.'

Sophy gave a disgusted snort. 'It isn't natural for him to be ashamed of your success to the point where he doesn't like people to know you're The Unicorn!'

Warm colour darkened Eve's cheeks. 'He isn't ashamed of my success,' she defended stiltedly. 'He's just trying to protect me.'

'From what?' the other woman challenged, her beautiful head thrown back.

Eve shook her head. 'You wouldn't understand.'

Auburn brows rose over snapping green eyes. 'Do you?' Sophy drawled hardly.

Eve gave a heavy sigh. There had been a continuing argument between Paul and Sophy in recent months, because Paul, as her adviser and lawyer, refused to let Sophy launch the publicity campaign concerning The Unicorn that would, without it actually coming to the point of revealing her true identity, seriously endanger her anonymity.

The Unicorn, because of the subject of her paintings, had been a name she and Sophy had come up with for her during that first frank discussion about her work. And while the name, coupled with her work, had added a certain amount of interest during the early years, Sophy now insisted that it was no longer necessary, claimed it would only add to the success of her work if it should come out that The Unicorn was a woman, and not the man everyone had so readily assumed it to be.

Paul insisted as strongly that her identity remain a secret. And so the argument went on, with Paul coming to the point where he had advised Eve not to take part in the winter exhibition at all if Sophy couldn't do what they asked.

'Let's not talk about that any more today, Sophy,' she dismissed wearily. 'I hope you managed to placate that man Adam after the rash promise you had made him,' she added teasingly.

'I only told him The Unicorn would be at the party; it was up to him to discover who that was. Besides,' the other woman gave a wicked grin, 'he was so relieved to learn that Paul *wasn't* The Unicorn that I didn't need to placate him at all!'

'Sophy——' Eve chided wryly.

'Well, it's true,' Sophy insisted with wide-eyed innocence. 'He almost got down and kissed my feet when I assured him Paul was telling the truth.'

She couldn't help smiling; Sophy really was outrageous! 'Who is he, anyway?' she queried lightly, deciding she might just as well ignore the other woman's sarcasm at Paul's expense; Sophy took no notice of her reproof, anyway!

'A successful entrepreneur, worth millions,' Sophy confided. 'And he also owns one of the most prestigious galleries in New York,' she added excitedly, her veneer of bored cynicism slipping in her genuine enthusiasm for the subject.

It was when Sophy was like this that Eve could see the side of her that Patrick obviously knew and loved so well. A confirmed, single-minded career-woman until Patrick had come into her life, there was obviously something within him that was able to reach into the softer core of her, some quality that only Patrick possessed; this more endearing side of Sophy was certainly never in evidence when Paul was around. If it were, they possibly wouldn't argue quite so much!

'And he's very interested in the The Unicorn paintings the gallery owns,' Sophy continued triumphantly. 'Informed me that he has his own private collection back in New York.'

His admiration for Eve's work had been more than obvious a couple of evenings ago, but nevertheless it shook her slightly to think of him owning any of her work; the paintings were, after all, private pieces of herself she had put on to canvas. He had been right when he'd said her work came from her heart and soul, and each painting was a labour of love.

'Apparently he always has at least two pieces of your work on display at his gallery,' Sophy confided with enthusiasm. 'In fact, he wanted me to approach you about taking your winter exhibition over to New York. With Patrick and me working on a commission and overseeing the project, of course.'

'Of course,' Eve said drily.

But she couldn't help feeling pleasure in the compliment she had just been given. Each painting she did *was* a labour of love, and when it left her studio to be sold at Sophy's gallery it went with great reluctance on Eve's part to let that part of herself go. She had often wondered what sort of person, just who, would claim her latest and most precious 'child'; each successive painting had always become the most precious.

Much as it made her feel slightly uncomfortable to think of the man Adam owning several parts of her inner self in that way, she also knew instinctively that the paintings would be cherished by him, that despite being a businessman he was able to appreciate the emotional value of her work and not just the financial; and so many of the buyers seemed to be concerned purely with the financial nowadays.

'And there's more,' Sophy added, with a gleam of laughter in her eyes.

Eve instinctively distrusted that gleam. 'Oh?' she prompted warily.

'Mm,' the other woman said teasingly. 'He told me the two of you never had got around to introducing yourselves properly the other evening.'

'It didn't seem necessary, the fact that we're called Adam and Eve amused him enough,' she recalled with a heavy sigh.

Sophy chuckled. 'That's because he had the added insight of knowing his full name is Adam *Gardener*!' she announced with great enjoyment.

'It couldn't be!' Eve groaned, briefly closing her eyes, shaking her head as if to shut out the awful coincidence of that name.

'It is,' the other woman laughed softly. 'Think how much more amused he would have been if he had known he was talking to Eve *Eden*!'

It didn't even bear thinking about!

'What on earth were our parents thinking of when they named the two of us?' she gasped.

'Well, certainly not that you would ever meet each other!' Sophy was obviously enjoying herself immensely—at their expense.

And why shouldn't she? Good heavens, Adam Gardener and Eve Eden—it was too ridiculous to even think about!

'Well, at least that isn't likely to happen again.' Thank goodness. What a topic for conversation they would be if the people she knew should ever realise Adam's full name and its significance to hers. Goodness knew, her name alone had been a source of amusement for years; the two together would be just too much.

'If we do go into collaboration with him over an exhibition in New York, he will obviously want to meet you,' Sophy pointed out practically.

Eve shook her head very firmly. 'You know very well that I never travel.'

Sophy's mouth tightened. 'That's only because you've allowed——'

'Besides,' she cut in determinedly, wanting to avoid Sophy saying anything further that was detrimental to Paul, knowing the other woman usually lost no opportunity to criticise him, even if it wasn't always valid.

She simply didn't want to travel, it certainly had nothing whatsoever to do with Paul's aversion to her becoming involved with the artistic set that could become such a threat to their privacy.

'I'm just too busy working with my grandmother on the arrangements for the wedding in September.' Not that that was really taking up so much of her time; it was only going to be a small affair, with close family and a few friends.

And, if there was still this animosity between Paul and Sophy at that time, she had the feeling he was going to insist Sophy and Patrick not be included in the latter. It was going to be a serious bone of contention between them.

Sophy arched mocking brows. 'Is September when Paul has decided the wedding is to be?'

She gave a weary sigh. 'That's when *we* have decided it's to be, yes.'

The other woman gave a sceptical snort. 'But I have no doubt the date fits in very nicely with Paul's schedule.'

'Well, of course it does.' Eve was becoming more than a little irritable now. 'As the wedding can really be at any time, there would be no point in arranging it for when it's completely inconvenient for everyone involved.'

'September suits you too, does it?' Sophy derided drily.

'Sophy, I know you and Paul don't get on, but——'

'*That* has to be the understatement of the year!' the other woman scorned.

'—but he is the man I love and intend to marry,' Eve finished firmly, glaring fiercely.

Sophy was unaffected by that glare. 'More's the pity.' She looked totally disheartened by the prospect, even lacking her usual grace of movement as she dropped down into an armchair. 'OK, I'm sorry.' She waved an elegantly long hand dismissively. 'But the man can be so bloody-minded.'

Eve smiled without rancour at this familiar accusation. 'You just don't like him because he doesn't readily agree with what you want.'

Sophy drew in a ragged breath, raising sleepy lids. 'Is that what you think?' she frowned.

'I know it,' she chided indulgently.

Her friend just looked at her for several seconds. 'If you say so,' she finally sighed. 'So what are the chances of the two of you coming to dinner this week?' she drawled in a bored voice.

Eve smiled. 'You didn't have to come all the way over here to ask me that; a telephone call would have sufficed,' she said tauntingly.

Sophy had too much self-confidence and outright nerve to look even the slightest bit disconcerted by the sarcasm. 'I wasn't about to waste this opportunity to talk to you about the exhibition we want to set up for you this winter——'

'I didn't think you needed an excuse to do that,' she teased, moving to look out of the huge studio window, loving, as always, the utter peace and tranquillity that met her gaze. The work she had been able to have done on this old family house was the biggest reward she had received from her painting, and from the legacy she had had from her parents on her twenty-first birthday that had allowed her to concentrate fully on that career that had brought so many rewards.

Her gaze softened with love as her grandmother glanced up from where she was working on her rose garden to see her standing at the third-floor window, and the old lady straightened to wave happily in the sunshine.

Her grandmother had been the most important person in Eve's life after the death of her parents twenty years ago, when Eve was only six and Evelyn Ashton was already in her early fifties.

The elderly woman hadn't hesitated about taking over the care of both of her young granddaughters after the road accident that had robbed her of her only two children, her son and his wife, and her daughter and her husband, the four returning from a weekend in the country when their car had lost control and gone over the side of a bridge. Four-year-old Marina and six-year-old Eve had been left orphaned after the crash.

Ashton House had become a haven for Eve and her young cousin, and Evelyn Ashton a source of never-ending love. It hadn't been until Eve was in her teens that she had realised her only two children's lives wasn't the only price her grandmother had paid all those years ago; because of some unsound investments on the family's behalf by her only son, investments he hadn't had time to correct before his untimely death, everything but the family home had been sacrificed, too. And the house, far from being the palatial place that Eve had always imagined it to be, was run-down and very much in need of repair.

The money her parents had left in trust for her until she was twenty-one hadn't been enough to carry out all the work that needed doing, and her grandmother had insisted that she use part of it to pursue the career that might otherwise have been denied her. The first thing she had done when she'd begun to earn money from her paintings was to finish restoring the house to its former glory; Ashton House was now the home her grandmother could be proud of.

'She's a wonderful old lady,' Sophy murmured appreciatively at Eve's side, having noiselessly crossed the room to join her at the window.

Eve glanced round at her. 'I wouldn't let her hear the old part of that statement,' she said drily.

The other woman grimaced. 'Now there's someone I *do* respect.'

Eve continued to gaze fondly at her grandmother. 'She's particularly happy at the moment because Marina is coming home for a few days this weekend.'

'Your lovely cousin has found time from her busy social schedule to visit the woman who brought her up?' Sophy said scoffingly. 'How nice!'

Eve sighed, shaking her head. 'There aren't many people you do like, are there?'

The other woman shrugged. 'I like you, I like your grandmother, I even like Adam Gardener— and not just because of the good he could do your career and my gallery,' she drawled, without apology for her earlier remarks about Eve's cousin. 'I have little time for fools.' She gave a graceful shrug.

The mention of his name had brought the image of Adam Gardener to mind; somehow she had the feeling he didn't suffer fools gladly, either. He certainly hadn't suffered what he considered to be her foolish behaviour without comment!

'Dinner tomorrow,' Sophy announced briskly. 'Can that be arranged? I know you have to talk it over with Paul before making any definite arrangements, but are there any other plans he can put up as a valid excuse *not* to come?'

'I doubt it,' Eve said drily. 'But of course, I'll have to check with him first.'

'I never expected anything else.' The other woman nodded briskly. 'Call me as soon as you know for definite. I'll take it the two of you are coming until I hear otherwise.'

Eve was still smiling ruefully to herself a few minutes later as she went outside to join her grandmother; it was typical of Sophy's arrogance that she *assumed* she and Paul would be present at her dinner party 'unless she heard otherwise'. No wonder the other woman always succeeded in rubbing Paul up the wrong way; he *hated* it when people made arrangements for him without even the politeness of consulting him on it.

Her grandmother straightened as she saw Eve approaching; she was a tall, grey-haired figure with a deceptively stern façade, behind which lay a mischievous nature, a fact Eve and Marina had quickly learnt once they had come to live with her. 'Sophy on her usual form?' she said with affection, the respect between the two women definitely mutual.

'When is she anything else?' Eve murmured derisively, running a caressing hand across a perfectly formed pink rose. This garden was her grandmother's pride and joy, her 'bolt-hole when caring for two small girls', she had claimed teasingly when Eve and Marina were a lot younger, and she spent hours caring for the beautiful blossoms, a fact reflected in their perfection.

'Marriage has softened her a little,' Eve's grandmother excused. 'I can remember a time when she was very brittle and cynical.'

'According to Paul, she still is—among other things,' Eve sighed, a little weary after this last conversation of this constant battle between the two of them.

Sophy might be the daughter of an old friend of her grandmother's, but Paul was the son of her grandmother's lawyer; he had taken over his father's law office when Edgar Lester had died two years ago, and Eve knew that her grandmother had affection for both Paul and Sophy, a fact that was reflected in her reply.

'It wouldn't do if we were all the same, darling.' She smiled reassuringly, patting her hand. 'Paul is uneasy around Sophy because she is what she is, but he loves *you* for the same reason.'

Because she was what she was.

According to Adam Gardener, she was little more than a 'walking doormat' waiting to be walked over. A frown marred her brow as thought of the other man came unbidden to her mind for the second time that day.

But how could she help but occasionally think about a man she now knew as Adam Gardener— when her own name was *Eve Eden*?

'You're sure he isn't just being selfish again?' Sophy sceptically voiced her disbelief while Patrick took Eve's jacket.

Eve gave the other woman a reproving look from turquoise eyes, her dress a perfect match for their colour; it was high-necked and sleeveless, somehow all the more sexy because of that. 'I doubt he had the client call him on purpose,' she taunted.

'I wouldn't put that past him.' Sophy put her arm companionably through Eve's as they walked through to the lounge of the couple's elegantly furnished apartment. 'Anything to avoid spending time with me!'

Paul had telephoned Eve only minutes before he was due to pick her up to drive them both to the

O'Donnells for dinner, to tell her that a client needed to see him urgently and that he was going to be indefinitely delayed.

She had to admit that the thought of him having used an imaginary appointment with a client to opt out of the dinner he had only agreed to go to for her sake, had briefly—disloyally—crossed her own mind earlier. He had been so against coming here for the dinner when she'd broached the subject with him, so perhaps she could be excused that one little doubt, especially as she had dismissed the disloyal thought only seconds after it had entered her mind. Paul wouldn't be that small-minded; he did everything he could to try and please her, always showering her with gifts, his thoughtfulness undoubted. Sophy just didn't understand him.

'Leave the subject alone, darling,' Patrick advised softly from behind the two of them. 'We should be using this opportunity to try and persuade Eve into agreeing to just thinking about a New York exhibition.'

'A lot of good talking to her about it will do if Paul doesn't agree,' Sophy scoffed disgustedly as her husband crossed the room to pour them all a drink.

Patrick gave his wife a silencing glance—and it was evidence of Sophy's love for him that she actually took notice of the warning—albeit with tight-lipped self-control.

Patrick's gaze softened as he handed Eve the martini she had asked for. 'We would both like you to do this exhibition in New York because we feel it would be the final burst your career needs,' he told her gently. 'Not because we want any personal glory from it—no matter what might have been said to the contrary,' he added with an affectionate smile at Sophy.

Eve sighed. 'An exhibition isn't what's really the problem——'

'Paul is the prob—— Sorry.' Sophy held up defensive hands as Patrick flashed her a warning glare. 'I can't help it if I think all this secrecy is a waste of a beautiful woman,' she defended defiantly, exceptionally lovely herself tonight in a figure-hugging dress that showed the perfection of her slender figure.

'As I recall, *you* were the one who decided The Unicorn was a great name for an artist, and thought the elusiveness of the person behind the paintings was a great publicity angle,' Eve reminded drily.

'That was because I forgot that, according to legend, the Unicorn was so damned elusive he became extinct!' Sophy snorted, undaunted.

Eve couldn't help but chuckle at her friend's utter despair with her attitude towards her anonymity; it was so uncharacteristic of the self-confident Sophy that she couldn't do anything else!

It was Sophy's undoing that Patrick began to chuckle, too, her own grin one of self-mockery.

'Why do I bother, right?' she grimaced, with a careless shrug of her shoulders. 'But if I didn't——' She broke off as the doorbell rang loudly.

'That will be Paul.' Eve instantly brightened at the thought of the man she loved. 'He must have finished earlier than expected and decided to join us, after all.'

'How nice!' Sophy murmured sarcastically as she moved to answer the door.

'I'd apologise for her, except that I know she's just as likely to come back in here and be just as rude all over again—but to Paul's face this time!' Patrick muttered impatiently. 'I can't spend the rest of my life apologising for her outrageous out-spokenness.' He shook his head.

Just as Eve, supposedly, couldn't spend the rest of *her* life 'apologising for being alive'. Once again Adam Gardener's hurtful remarks came back to disturb her peace of mind.

She had thought back to their conversation several times since Saturday evening, probably because no one—not even Sophy—had spoken to her in quite that forthright way before. Lord knew what he would have to say to her if he should ever realise she was The Unicorn, the artist he so obviously ad-mired, but also a woman he thought in need of care and protection from herself!

She gave a small gasp as, as if her thought of him had conjured him up, she looked up to find Adam Gardener entering the room behind Sophy!

'Look who just happened to be passing,' the other woman announced brightly to no one in particular.

On his way to another engagement if his dark evening suit was anything to go by, his rakishly good looks as attractive as before, his hair looking more golden than ever tonight, as if he had spent his time between Saturday night and now just lazing in the sunshine. The fitness of his wide shoulders, flatness of his tapered waist, and his muscled thighs contradicted that impression as something he did often.

Remembering his blunt criticism of her the other evening, Eve could only hope his visit was to be a short one, although it didn't look as if it would be *too* short, as Patrick offered him a drink and he accepted. Sophy took the opportunity to excuse herself to go and check on dinner.

Eve felt only dismay as Adam Gardener crossed the room, lowering his six-feet-two-inch frame down on to the sofa beside her, *very close* beside her.

'So we meet again, Eve Eden,' he drawled, the laughter very much back in dark brown eyes.

'So we do—Adam Gardener,' she returned caustically, determined not to be disconcerted by this man as she had been the last time they met.

He glanced across the room, to where Sophy had disappeared through a doorway into the kitchen. 'I see our hostess had been busy talking to you, too,' he mocked, dark, compelling eyes returning to her face. 'But I think there's something else you should know about me,' he added conspiratorially.

'Oh, yes?' she prompted disinterestedly.

'Hm.' He nodded, bending closer to her. 'I think you should know right now that I didn't "just happen to be passing" anywhere,' he told her softly. 'I was specifically invited here tonight by Sophy.' He sat back slightly, his eyes narrowed. 'It looks as if our hostess may be up to a little matchmaking between the two of us,' he informed her drily.

CHAPTER THREE

SO MUCH for her determination not to let him disconcert her a second time!

It took her a couple of seconds to recover from it this time. But *only* a couple of seconds!

'Don't be ridiculous,' she snapped indignantly. 'Sophy knows I'm shortly to be married.'

Adam nodded, not in the least perturbed by her show of anger. 'I'm sure she does—but her opinion of your boyfriend appears to be about as high as mine,' he said dismissively.

'Sophy *has* been talking,' Eve bit out tautly, eyes blazing.

He shook his head. 'In this case, Sophy didn't need to say a thing; I could tell how she felt about your Paul by her attitude towards him. A very forthright lady, is Sophy O'Donnell,' he added, with obvious admiration.

'Too forthright and honest to be involved in what you're implying,' she agreed agitatedly. 'Besides, Paul was supposed to be here with me tonight,' she reminded triumphantly.

Dark blond brows rose as Adam looked about the room pointedly. 'Then why isn't he?' he finally drawled.

Colour darkened her cheeks. 'He's been held up unexpectedly at his office with a client,' she explained defensively.

'Of course.' Adam nodded mockingly. 'He's a lawyer, isn't he?'

'As opposed to being an artist, yes,' Eve told him challengingly.

His mouth twisted. 'I'm glad that particular nightmare didn't come true.'

She drew in a ragged breath. 'Mr Gardener——'

'Adam,' he put in softly. 'Please call me Adam—Eve.'

Adam and Eve. Certainly, they were nothing like that other Adam and Eve; a more unsuited pair than Adam Gardener and herself was unlikely to be seen for a long time to come!

'Very well—Adam,' she conceded stiltedly. 'But I really don't think you have any reason to be abusive about Paul in this way.'

His darkly intense gaze didn't waver for a second. 'You don't?'

Her mouth firmed at his arrogance. Damn the man, he had no *right*! 'You——'

'Dinner is served,' Sophy announced in a lightly teasing voice.

Eve looked up at the other woman dazedly as she interrupted the heated conversation, her cheeks feeling as if they were aflame as she realised the reason for Sophy's mockery; Patrick had been standing idly by for the last few minutes with the whisky and ice Adam had requested, completely unnoticed by either of them. A fact that Sophy viewed with speculative amusement.

Eve stood up determinedly. 'I'll help you carry things through.' Her steady gaze dared Sophy to refuse that help.

She should have known the other woman was too self-confident to even look mildly uncomfortable about the subterfuge she had used concerning Adam's presence here and obvious intention of staying for dinner, Sophy merely giving her a cheeky grin as she preceded her through to the kitchen.

'Sophy——'

'Fascinating man, isn't he?' the other woman announced as she picked up the ornate soup tureen. She paused at the door, auburn brows raised mockingly. 'At least, you seemed to find him so.'

Eve stood in the middle of the kitchen and counted to ten while the door swung shut behind the other woman. She didn't like this situation one little bit; she had the definite feeling Adam was right about Sophy's intentions, and that the other woman's dislike of Paul was making her behave in this shameless way. Eve just hoped Paul would be able to get away and arrive soon so that he could put an end to this stupidity; she very much doubted she was going to get any help from Adam Gardener in that direction!

In that she was proved very much correct, as Adam made a point through dinner of drawing her into the conversation, constantly prompting her to talk about herself, to tell him of what little family she had, to discuss the job she had continued to do at the local library despite her other career, simply because she enjoyed meeting and talking with people. Painting was a very solitary occupation.

Her uneasiness with the situation turned to apprehensive qualms when Patrick answered the telephone after the meal, then told her the call was for her—from Paul.

'Take the call in our bedroom,' Patrick offered softly as he saw her agitation.

She gladly accepted the invitation, carefully avoiding compelling dark eyes as she crossed the lounge to firmly close the bedroom door behind her.

Adam Gardener had the gift of making her feel totally uncomfortable; he wouldn't allow her the privilege of drifting into the background as she liked to do, always having preferred to be the listener rather than the centre of attention.

She took a deep, controlling breath before lifting the receiver of the extension, forcing her voice to be bright and untroubled. 'Hello, darling,' she greeted smoothly. 'Nearly finished?'

'No, I'm not,' Paul's abrupt answer instantly dashed her hopes that he was on his way to join her. 'What are you doing at the O'Donnells' after all?' he added impatiently. 'I telephoned Ashton House to talk to you just now, and your grandmother gave me your message that I was to join you when I had finished. I thought we had agreed earlier that we would cancel the dinner for tonight and make other arrangements?'

Eve sat down on the edge of the quilt-covered bed, the purple and lilac décor in here as flamboyant as the rest of the house. 'It was such short notice for us to cancel, so I——'

'It was utterly ridiculous for you to go to the O'Donnells' alone,' Paul cut in irritably.

'A friend of Sophy and Patrick's called unexpectedly and stayed for the meal, so we weren't an odd number,' she quickly defended, and then wished she hadn't as she guessed the questions that would follow such a leading statement.

'Male or female?' Paul queried suspiciously.

Usually this protective part of Paul's nature made her feel cherished and loved, but tonight, after another emotional battering from Adam Gardener, it just made her feel weary. The last thing she felt like doing just now was answering a lot of questions from Paul on the 'unexpected guest', especially as he had already met the other man—and their dislike had been mutual.

'Female,' she heard herself reply—and then wondered why on earth she had told such a lie.

She could never remember lying to Paul about anything before! It was no good telling herself she hadn't felt like going into lengthy explanations; the truth of the matter was that she had just *lied*, blatantly. And it was going to cause more trouble than it was worth to tell Paul the truth now; she could hardly say, Oh, no, sorry—it was a man, after all! What on earth was happening to her?

'Nevertheless,' Paul answered sharply, 'I'm sure the O'Donnells would have understood our need to cancel dinner tonight if you had just explained the situation to them.'

Sophy wouldn't have understood any such thing, she would have been full of scathing comments, although that wasn't the reason Eve had decided to come to dinner on her own; she had just hoped Paul wouldn't be delayed too long by business and they could still have had most of the evening together with Sophy and Patrick.

Paul couldn't possibly realise how much she wished she *had* taken heed of his suggestion now and made their excuses!

'Never mind, darling,' she dismissed lightly. 'When do you think you might be able to get away?' She would arrange to meet him at home if it were to be soon; she didn't want him coming here and finding her out in her stupid, ridiculous lie.

'Not soon enough tonight for us to meet,' he told her irritably, dashing her hopes that they might salvage something of the evening, after all. 'For some reason, Daniel Wall has decided he wants to review his will this evening,' he muttered. 'Forget I mentioned who the client is—although I know that isn't really necessary.' He sighed heavily.

She certainly wouldn't mention Daniel Wall's name to anyone as the client Paul was spending the evening with, but there was no way she could forget

he had been the one to delay Paul tonight—or that
he was a very good friend of Patrick's! The idea
that Sophy *was* matchmaking between herself and
Adam Gardener was now more than a 'feeling'.

'I'd better not keep you from him any longer,'
Eve said distractedly, more than a little annoyed
with Sophy for creating this crazy situation. She
was in love with Paul, and didn't need the com-
plication of a man like Adam Gardener disrupting
her life. 'Will you be over to the house tomorrow
evening?'

'Your grandmother has already invited me to
dinner. Apparently Marina has managed to get
away a few days earlier than expected, and there's
to be a family dinner party to celebrate,' Paul explained derisively.

Sophy wasn't alone in her opinion of Marina; it
was probably the only thing she and Paul had in
common, and even that was probably one they
wished they didn't have!

In her career as an actress, Marina could sometimes be a little thoughtless in her actions, a little
selfish, but there was no malice in her. The only
thing that did bother Eve about Marina's behaviour was the way she occasionally let their
grandmother down; but, as the elderly lady affectionately accepted the thoughtlessness, Eve tended
to do the same thing.

'That will be nice.' She smiled at the thought of
seeing her cousin again; Ashton House was never
dull when Marina was about. 'I'll see you to-

morrow, then. And don't work too hard tonight,' she added teasingly.

'I don't think you should stay too much longer at the O'Donnells',' Paul advised lightly. 'After all, you do have to go to work in the morning.'

She felt warmed by his concern for her. 'I'll be leaving soon,' she promised him warmly. 'Take care, darling. I love you.'

'Don't let Sophy talk you into anything,' he warned harshly. 'You know how damned pushy she can be. And I don't want——'

'Paul, this is a dinner party,' Eve soothed.

'That isn't likely to bother Sophy,' he scorned knowingly. 'Even with one of her friends there.'

The mention of that 'friend' sobered Eve, brought vividly to mind compelling brown eyes.

'I had better rejoin the others,' she told Paul distractedly. 'And don't worry,' she added teasingly, 'I won't let Sophy talk me into having my photograph as The Unicorn splashed all over the front page of the daily newspapers!'

'I'm glad you find it all so amusing, Eve,' Paul reproved stiffly, obviously not in the least amused himself. 'I know how much you value your career, but it isn't going to do my future ambitions in politics any good if your secret is made public——'

'Paul——'

'—especially after what Ellington-James's wife did to him at the height of his career. She walked out on him and his young daughter seemingly without a backward glance. You know as well as I

do that in political circles image is everything. As
for the voters, they aren't likely to choose a
man——'

'Paul, I was only joking about having my picture
in the newspapers,' Eve cut in exasperatedly. 'You
know I have no intention of being involved in any
sort of publicity.'

'Don't even joke about something like that.' The
horror could be heard in his voice. 'The subject
makes me lose all my sense of humour.'

'All right, darling,' she acknowledged affectionately. 'But Sophy hasn't even brought up the subject
of the winter exhibition.' Lately!

'I don't like the sound of that . . .'

'Oh, Paul, you're just being silly now.' She sighed
her impatience with the subject. 'Go and finish your
meeting with Daniel Wall and forget all about this
dinner party.' Which was exactly what she intended
doing when *she* got home! 'I'll call you tomorrow,'
she promised.

'Very well,' he accepted reluctantly. 'But do remember what I said about Sophy.'

Eve didn't rejoin the others in the lounge straight
away, for she was a little disturbed by the discord
between herself and Paul. In fact, there seemed to
have been several such incidents since she had met
Adam Gardener three days earlier. The sooner she
persuaded Sophy to give up her ridiculous schemes
the better; maybe then she could get back to living
quietly, without the sort of exposure being near

Adam Gardener threatened. She needed to have a serious talk with Sophy about several things!

'That's a big frown for such a little face,' remarked a voice that was becoming all too familiar.

Eve looked up sharply to find Adam standing across the room from her, his gaze warmly caressing.

'You didn't have to come looking for me,' she told him agitatedly. 'I was just about to come through to the lounge and rejoin you all.'

'There's no rush.' He crossed the room to drop down on the side of the bed beside her, the dipping of the mattress meaning she also dipped towards his heavier weight. 'Boyfriend been giving you a hard time?' he sympathised.

'Certainly not.' She stood up abruptly. 'Paul has just been delayed longer than he anticipated, that's all. I'm naturally disappointed that he isn't going to be able to join me.'

'Naturally,' Adam agreed as he too stood up, instantly dwarfing the room.

And she had claimed it was a female guest; anyone less effeminate she was unlikely to meet. And yet he wasn't chauvinistic either.

Eve gave him a condemning look; whether because he was once again being less than respectful about Paul, or because he intrigued her in spite of herself, she didn't want to know.

'I know your opinion of Paul isn't very high . . .'

'I've made no secret of that,' he derided.

'No, you haven't,' she snapped, anger as good a form of defence against this man as any other.

He held up his hands placatingly. 'All right, I'll lay off the boyfriend—for the moment,' he added provocatively, his gaze teasing. 'I actually came through to ask you if you could drive me back to my hotel when you leave; Sophy told me it's on your way home.'

Sophy would! Beside the fact that the other woman's suggestion had put her in an awkward position, it had also effectively put a stop to her confronting Sophy with her machinations once Adam had left. Clever, clever Sophy...

'If Sophy said so, then I'm sure it must be true,' she bit out.

Adam's mouth quirked. 'What's that saying? I'd like to be a "fly on the wall" the next time you talk to Sophy alone.'

Eve relaxed slightly; it was a little difficult to do anything else with this mischievously mocking man. 'I can assure you you wouldn't,' she drawled. 'It's going to be a very one-sided conversation—for once!'

His grin widened. 'I like you when you're like this... Sorry,' he grimaced as she instantly stiffened. 'If you would rather not give her the satisfaction of knowing she has successfully staged this, too, I can always get a cab.'

'Staged this, too'? Did Adam realise the lengths she believed Sophy to have gone to on his behalf tonight? The open amusement in his ruggedly handsome face said a definite no; this man didn't need anyone's help where women were concerned!

'I wouldn't give her the satisfaction of thinking I was afraid to drive you home,' she said determinedly. 'Which I'm certainly not,' she added firmly at his questioningly raised brows. 'Besides which,' she added mockingly, 'it will be worth it just to see her face the next time we meet, when I refuse to tell her all the details!'

'Will there be any "details" *not* to tell her?' Adam countered interestedly.

She gave him a warning look. 'No.'

'That's what I thought,' he sighed with exaggerated disappointment. 'Maybe we should just add to her curiosity by telling her we intend leaving now? That should have her guessing, when we've been alone in her bedroom all this time.'

My goodness, so they had! She hated to think what construction the other woman would put on *that*.

To add to her embarrassment, Eve heard a delighted chuckle from behind her as she hurried from the bedroom, her cheeks burning fiery red as Sophy and Patrick turned to them both with mocking enquiry.

'Eve and I thought we might leave now.' Adam spoke before she had a chance.

She turned to him with a furiously warning glare, forcing a tight smile to her lips as her gaze returned to the other couple. 'Paul isn't going to be able to get away at all tonight, after all,' she excused lightly.

'That's no reason for you to have to go just yet,' Patrick told her softly, his expression sympathetic to the situation his wife had undoubtedly created.

'We both have an early start in the morning.' Once again, Adam was the one to do the talking for both of them.

And while Eve was quite happy, loving him as she did, to let Paul make decisions for them both, she certainly wasn't willing to let Adam Gardener do the same thing.

Adam Gardener—oh lord, the very name still gave her the shudders!

'I really do have to go now,' she put in firmly. 'And as I'm giving Adam a lift to his hotel . . .' she added with a warning look at Sophy, the other woman looking back unrepentantly.

'Yes, we really must be on our way,' Adam added provocatively.

Sophy stood up slowly. 'Well, if you *really* must,' she remarked, her eyes gleaming her satisfaction with the arrangement.

'Patrick has himself a tiger by the tail,' Adam chuckled once the two of them were outside and crossing the road to where Eve's car was parked.

'He doesn't seem to mind,' Eve dismissed unsympathetically, more than a little put out with both Sophy and Patrick. Maybe if Patrick tried a little harder to curb Sophy's mischief-making . . .

At the very least there was going to be a very heated telephone line between Eve's home and the

O'Donnells' in the near future—the *very* near future!

Adam grinned. 'Life sure can't be dull with a woman like that. Although *my* life has been far from monotonous since I met you on Saturday night.' He gave Eve a pointed glance.

Her mouth firmed at his flirtatious manner. Sophy and her ideas! 'This is just a lift back to your hotel, Mr Gardener,' she bit out.

'I never thought it was anything else,' he returned innocently, too innocently for Eve's peace of mind.

'I'm going to be married in a few months' time,' she reminded crossly.

'What's that saying? The deed isn't done until the ring is on the lady's finger?' He quirked dark blond brows.

Eve's eyes widened. 'I think you just made that "saying" up!'

He grinned again. 'I think I did, too—but it doesn't make it any less true.'

'Shall we just get this journey over with, Mr Gardener?' she snapped impatiently.

'Certainly, Miss Eden,' he mocked. 'I—— What's this?' He frowned his puzzlement as she held out her car keys to him so that he could get in behind the wheel.

The passing over of the keys had been a completely automatic gesture on her part. 'I'm sorry, I forgot you weren't used to driving on our roads,' she said ruefully, unlocking the car doors for them both.

'I've driven myself in England many times,' he shrugged off the statement, still frowning as he gingerly eased his bulk into the small white sports car.

The purchase of the car had been an adolescent weakness of hers that she hadn't been able to resist once she had the money to indulge it. But it was obviously a completely unsuitable vehicle for a man of Adam Gardener's stature; he looked most uncomfortable beside her as she climbed in behind the wheel, their elbows knocking together.

'Do I take it from the offer that Paul usually drives your car for you when you're together?' Adam queried softly.

'Yes, he——' Eve broke off as she realised the incredulity behind his question. 'There's nothing wrong with a man wanting to do the driving.' Her cheeks were flushed as she was once again put in the position of having to defend Paul.

'Not if you're a one hundred per cent male chauvinist, no,' he acknowledged drily. 'Tell me, does he ever let you behind the wheel of the BMW I noticed he was driving the other evening?'

She breathed in deeply. 'I'm not used to driving a car of that size.'

'Has he ever offered to let you try?' Adam persisted.

She gave him an impatient glare. 'Do you ever let women drive your car?'

'Frequently,' he drawled, pausing before adding softly, 'I've always thought it says a lot about a couple's—intimate relationship.'

'Driving?' she gasped.

'Who does it.' He nodded. 'It's a question of who is in control, and I've always believed——'

'I don't think I care to hear what you believe on the subject,' she cut in tautly.

'Possibly not,' he conceded gently. 'But just for the record, *you* could drive my car any time you wanted.'

There wasn't a lot she could say to that! But the conversation had disturbed her so much, she crunched the gears in her agitation.

Adam arched mocking brows at her. 'Maybe I should have done the driving, after all.'

After the double-edged conversation they had just had on the subject, *never*!

'That won't be necessary,' she told him firmly, determined not to make another mistake in her driving during the short drive to his hotel.

She also didn't speak. This man deliberately went out of his way to be rude to her. The suggestive latter part of the conversation aside, why on earth shouldn't Paul be the one to do the driving when they went out together? Thousands of other men in the world did the same thing every day of their lives, and yet Adam Gardener had to make it seem as if it were yet another black mark against Paul. In *his* opinion.

She didn't give a damn about his opinion!

'The lady doth protest too much, methinks,' popped unbidden into her mind.

Maybe she was being a little vehement about Adam Gardener and his outspoken views, but then, those views were of someone he didn't even know. Her grandmother simply hadn't brought her up to criticise someone she did know, let alone pass judgement on people she didn't know. Maybe if she had, Eve could have dispatched Adam with a few well-chosen words the first time they had met!

She forced herself to relax at the thought, knowing that her efforts to use those 'few well-chosen words' this evening had so far failed, so why blame herself for something she couldn't change?

'Would you like to come into one of the lounges for a drink?' he offered once she had halted her car, with some relief, outside his brightly illuminated hotel.

She gave him an openly incredulous look. Prolong this nightmare; he had to be joking!

'I guess not,' he drawled with amusement. 'I hope we meet again, Eve Eden. You don't need to tell me you wish the opposite.' He grinned unabashedly. 'Maybe I would feel the same way if the roles were reversed,' he conceded lightly.

Her mouth twisted derisively. 'That isn't ever likely to happen.'

'No,' he acknowledged thoughtfully, his gaze moving searchingly across her face, his smile tinged with sadness now. 'Don't be in too much of a hurry to dismiss me from your life, Eve,' he murmured softly. 'I'm a great believer in fate, and so I believe there has to be a reason for the two of us having met in this way.'

'Fate's malicious sense of humour, most probably,' she dismissed scornfully.

'Or its way of showing you that you're making a mistake marrying Paul,' Adam almost whispered the words. The two of them were suddenly locked in a tension-filled spell, their gazes enmeshed, seeming to reach into each other's souls.

'I happen to love him,' she snapped.

'Do you?' he frowned.

'Of course,' she said irritably, but she was still held captive by that spell, even felt herself moving slowly towards Adam at the same time as he seemed to move compulsively towards her.

And then the spell was harshly broken as the reflection in the driving mirror of the blaze of headlights of the car pulling in behind hers momentarily dazzled her. She shook her head dazedly, frowning as she saw it was taking Adam several seconds to regain his usual bantering manner, too.

'I'd better go,' he acknowledged ruefully. 'But I have a definite feeling you haven't seen the last of me.'

Eve sincerely hoped that she had! He upset her, disturbed her, and she didn't need that at this time in her life.

'Take care driving home,' he told her softly.

'Isn't that being chauvinistic and over-protective?' she derided, to hide the fact that the last few minutes had shaken her—badly.

'No,' he spoke softly, 'that's just me being concerned about someone I care for.'

'How on earth can you "care" for me?' Eve scorned. 'You don't know me any more than you know Paul.'

'I'll admit I haven't known you any longer, but then, that doesn't mean a thing. It only takes a second, Eve.'

She gave him a startled look. 'What does?'

He didn't answer immediately, just looked at her steadily. 'Knowing someone,' he finally answered—but Eve was left with the feeling it hadn't been what he meant to say at all.

'This is ridiculous,' she said firmly, refusing to think of that time only minutes ago when she had felt herself being drawn towards him. She loved Paul, always had, and no outspoken stranger was going to make any difference to that.

She pushed firmly to the back of her mind the fact that Adam was no longer a stranger at all, that the very nature of the man made that impossible.

'You probably have a wife in America and six children!' she said disgustedly.

He smiled. 'No wife. No children. And six of the latter at my age wouldn't be very fair to them; I'd be approaching fifty when the last one was born.'

'It wouldn't matter too much if your wife was younger than you,' Eve said without thinking, her cheeks burning as she saw the speculative look in his eyes.

'That's right,' he said softly. 'Although I'd be happy with just two—if you would.'

'Me? But——'

'I'm afraid your fate was sealed the moment I heard Paul Lester order you to stay put—I know, *you* didn't see it that way,' Adam drawled. 'But I know what I heard. I also know it made me want to tell him to go to hell, that you were with me. And I rarely, if ever, change my mind,' he added warningly. 'Besides,' he went on mockingly, 'we've already covered one of the subjects that a lot of couples argue about—how many children we intend having.' His eyes openly laughed at her.

'*We* aren't having any children at all,' she snapped, to hide how much his outrageous statement had affected her. The children they intended having was the one subject she and Paul tended to disagree about, Paul insisting they could give one child a better upbringing than two or three. Eve, although she saw the point of his claim, didn't approve of only children; they tended to either be very spoilt or very lonely. And neither was something she wanted for her child. It was something she hoped they could compromise on once they were married.

'We'll see,' Adam murmured softly. 'In the meantime, bear in mind the fact that if I had been averse to Sophy's plotting and planning for the two

of us, it would have been the simplest thing in the
world not to have turned up tonight.'

'You're as much a fantasiser as she is,' Eve bit
out tautly. 'And talking of fantasy, won't these
outrageous ideas you have about me distract you
from your real purpose, that of finding The
Unicorn?' Anything to divert his attention from the
two of them as a prospective couple!

He sighed. 'Sophy is being so close-mouthed
about him.' He shook his head. 'But don't worry,
I have another project moving ahead that should
get me that introduction.'

The exhibition in New York. After the ridiculous
claims he had already made concerning her this
evening, she definitely didn't dare run the risk of
him finding out *she* was The Unicorn; he would
probably carry her off there and then!

'I'm so glad,' she said with ill-concealed sarcasm.
'Now, I really must be going,' she told him
pointedly; he had been on the point of getting out
of the car for the last fifteen minutes, and had the
attentive doorman in a state of agitation with his
indecision.

'Remember what I've said,' he said as he finally
got out of the car.

How could she forget? She simply wasn't the type
to induce this state of impetuosity in complete
strangers. Now, if it had been Marina, beautiful,
flamboyant Marina, she might have understood it,
but she personally had always managed to remain
inconspicuous in a crowd. Maybe Adam Gardener

just had a warped sense of humour, although he had seemed perfectly serious at the time...

But she didn't have to see him again if she didn't want to, not once she had firmly told Sophy to behave herself in future!

But, to her dismay, Adam proved correct about it not being the last she saw of him! And he turned up again in the most unlikely place imaginable.

CHAPTER FOUR

By the time Marina arrived the next day, Eve had managed to push Adam Gardener's strangely disturbing comments from her mind. And, by the time the weekend came around and she had neither heard nor seen any more of him, she had managed to convince herself that she must have imagined the whole incident.

Almost.

It wasn't really all that easy convincing yourself that a man you hardly knew had calmly sat discussing with you the amount of children the two of you might have!

Sophy had once again been unrepentant about her part in things when Eve had telephoned her the day after the dinner party, the answering machine having conveniently been switched on at the apartment when Eve had tried to call the previous evening, immediately she got home. And any message she might care to 'leave after the tone' on that thing would have needed to have been highly censored!

She might just as well have saved her breath when she did finally manage to talk to the other woman; Sophy was convinced in her mind that Paul was all wrong for her, and that anything—or *anyone*—who could help Eve to realise that had Sophy's approval! She certainly saw nothing wrong in having suggested to Daniel Wall that the previous evening was as good a time as any to have his will reviewed considering his recent divorce, doing so with the full knowledge that such an occurrence would mean Paul couldn't join them for dinner.

By the time the call came to an end, Eve was feeling as frosty towards the other woman as Paul always was.

And she didn't see anything of Adam Gardener over the next few days, either. No unexpected appearances, and so no more caustic observations about her relationship with Paul.

She should be feeling happy. But she wasn't. Marina had come home in a terrible temper, the latest man in her life having let her down, in her estimation, by refusing to arrange for her to get the television role she had been interested in. The fact that so far Marina had only done a few commercials and a couple of very small parts in the theatre had no bearing on the subject as far as she was concerned.

Consequently, because her own world wasn't going the way she wanted it to, Marina was out to make trouble during her visit, deliberately antagonising Paul whenever she saw him, a fact he took great exception to. With good reason, Eve knew, but that didn't change the fact that she felt like a bone being pulled between the two of them, Marina playing on the sisterly affection there had always been between them for all she was worth. The way she was acting at the moment, Marina could have played the bitchy television role she had wanted blindfolded!

'I do so hope it's going to be a better day today.' Her grandmother frowned across the breakfast table to Eve on Saturday morning, Marina having her customary lie-in before Mrs Hodges took up her breakfast on a tray. Eve had never been able to understand how Marina got away with that one, considering all the other work Mrs Hodges had to do, but the housekeeper didn't seem to mind in the least.

Eve hoped today was going to be an improvement too; after three days of bickering between Marina and Paul every time they met, she was feeling decidedly ragged around the edges. 'Paul isn't coming over until this evening,' she said, as if that might help the situation.

'Then let's hope Marina doesn't decide to find someone else to take her temper out on.' Her grandmother shook her head ruefully. 'I can't understand it. I tried to bring the two of you up the same, to show the same amount of love and understanding to each of you, and yet I never have managed to completely master this temper of Marina's. Of course it was nowhere near as bad as this when she was a child. It seemed to surface more when she was in her teens, and even then I just thought it was a phase she was going through. She's been going through it for ten years now!' she said drily.

'Talking about me, Grandmother?' Marina swept into the room like a whirlwind, her attraction more of an impact than mere beauty alone.

Her hair fell in black, luxurious layers to just below her shoulders, dark blue eyes sparkling clearly in a perfect heart-shaped face; she was no taller than Eve, and yet somehow managed to appear so in the pencil-straight white trousers and white cotton sleeveless top.

'As a matter of fact, I was,' her grandmother answered sternly. 'Isn't it time you snapped out of this mood you've been in since you got here?'

'Oh, that.' Marina dismissed shruggingly, as if it were of no consequence any longer, bending across the table to pick an apple out of the fruit bowl standing in its centre. 'I've decided Gerald wasn't worth it, and that there will be other parts for me, better parts.' She bit cleanly into the apple with perfectly even white teeth. 'See you both later,' she announced happily around the mouthful of fruit.

'Where are you going now?' Her grandmother's exasperated question halted her in the doorway.

'Shopping,' Marina explained with relish, the front door closing noisily behind her seconds later as she left the house.

'Oh, dear,' sighed their grandmother wearily. 'I don't know which is worse, Marina morose and sulking, or in her usual bouncing mood and feeling like spending money!' She gazed after her youngest granddaughter worriedly.

Eve chuckled softly. 'At least she's more her normal self today.'

'Hm,' their grandmother acknowledged doubtfully.

Eve could sympathise with her grandmother's doubts; the last time Marina had decided to recover from a bad love-affair in the same way, her 'shopping spree' had amounted to the hundreds rather than tens. But, after all, it was her money to spend as she liked. As long as she didn't come and ask their grandmother for the loan of some money a couple of weeks later, as she had the last time!

With Marina out of the house and her grand-mother pottering about her beloved garden, Eve was able to put on her bikini and spend a peaceful morning sunbathing on the patio. It felt so wonder-ful to relax, to watch the butterflies flitting to and fro among the flowers, to listen to the bees buzzing lazily.

Rather like 'the calm before the storm', in fact!

One minute she was lying there, lazily contem-plating a pleasant evening with Paul, after all, now that Marina's mood had improved, and the next her dreamy state had been completely shattered.

'Hello, darling,' greeted a breezily familiar voice—the surprise of having Sophy disturb the utter tranquillity of the morning almost making Eve fall off her lounger.

She sat up hastily, pushing her sunglasses up into her hair to watch as the other woman strolled out of the house to join her.

'I hope you don't mind my coming out here like this.' Sophy smiled down at her, very beautiful in a flamboyant red and white silk sun-dress. 'Mrs Hodges told me the two of you were out here.' She gave Eve's grandmother a wave as she looked up and saw her with Eve.

Eve hadn't spoken to the other woman since their heated exchange on the telephone three days ago. 'If you've come here to apologise——'

'Certainly not,' Sophy dismissed briskly, dropping down on to the lounger next to Eve's as she watched Evelyn Ashton's progress towards them from the rose garden.

Eve frowned at the other woman. 'Then why *are* you here?' she finally asked when no explanation had been forthcoming.

'Why?' Sophy turned towards her, her own gaze puzzled now. 'But——'

'Sophy!' Eve's grandmother had finally reached them, and she greeted the other woman with pleasure. 'But where's Patrick?' she frowned.

'Parking the car and bringing in the luggage.' Sophy stood up to warmly kiss the older woman's cheek. 'Actually, he's taking rather a long time.' She was the one to frown now. 'Perhaps he can't find Mrs Hodges to tell him where we are, poor darling. I'll just go and get him.' She shot Eve a slightly triumphant look before going off in search of her husband.

Eve instantly mistrusted that look; what were the other couple doing here?

'Oh, dear, Eve, I am sorry I forgot to tell you about Sophy and Patrick coming,' her grandmother said worriedly as soon as Sophy disappeared inside the house. 'I've invited them to stay for the weekend, but with all this business with Marina the last few days and this morning, I'm afraid I forgot to mention it.' She shook her head. 'And it was really for Marina's sake that I invited them,' she added ruefully.

For the life of her, Eve couldn't see how inviting Sophy here was meant to be for Marina's benefit; the two women didn't get on at the best of times, let alone when Marina was going through one of her difficult moods. Considering the fact that their grandmother was also aware of that, she waited patiently for a further explanation of this rather unpleasant development. She wasn't feeling all that happy with Sophy herself at the moment, especially as Sophy still seemed so unconcerned with what she had done.

'I thought perhaps,' her grandmother continued distractedly, 'after this recent—upset in Marina's life, that she might be finding things a little dull around here, so I thought a weekend party while she's here might be a good idea. And Sophy just happened to telephone when I was going through the idea in my mind, and so... I know she and

Marina aren't the best of friends,' she grimaced. 'But you have to admit, life certainly isn't dull when the two of them are together!'

'No, I can't ever remember it being dull,' Eve acknowledged ruefully, sharing her grandmother's humour, at the same time remembering another person who had claimed that *his* life had been far from dull since he'd first met her...

Her grandmother brightened when Eve didn't immediately put a dampener on the idea. 'I did mean to talk to you about it this morning, but then Marina came in and mentioned going shopping, and—well, I got distracted.' She made a face.

'That happens to most people when Marina mentions going shopping.' Eve echoed the grimace.

'Yes, I—— Ah, here they come now.' She beamed at her guests over Eve's shoulder.

Eve wasn't really sure she was prepared yet to forget Sophy's part in the events of the last week, but with the other woman as a guest in the house she wasn't really going to have any choice in the matter; any strain between herself and Sophy would soon become apparent to her grandmother and, after the last few days they had had with Marina, she certainly had no intention of adding to the older woman's worries.

Nevertheless, she really wasn't prepared for the shock she received as she turned with a fatalistic sigh to greet Sophy and Patrick.

Adam Gardener strolled along at Patrick's side, a warmly sensual smile lighting his face as his gaze met and held Eve's stricken one.

What on earth was he doing here? Surely Sophy and Patrick hadn't ...

'Sophy mentioned that they had a weekend guest of their own,' her grandmother explained softly. 'So I told them to bring him along too; I said we have plenty of room. Actually, I thought he might help even the numbers up,' she confided ruefully. 'I'm rather glad I did invite him now, he looks a very personable young man. At least Marina should be pleased!'

'A very personable young man' hardly described Adam Gardener in Eve's opinion! And what could her grandmother mean about Marina being pleased he was here? Good lord, her grandmother didn't really intend to partner Marina and Adam off for the weekend, did she? Adam had the ability to demolish the flirtatious Marina with a few cutting remarks!

But maybe he wouldn't want to; after all, Marina was very beautiful. And her cousin was also completely available to return that attraction ...

Unlike Eve, herself.

Why did these strange thoughts come into her mind whenever Adam Gardener was in the vicinity? She didn't *want* to be available to return Adam Gardener's attraction!

While she had stood by like someone suffering from shell-shock—as indeed, she felt—Sophy had effected the introductions, Adam smiling with lazy charm as he greeted Eve's grandmother.

'But how incredible,' her grandmother was saying dazedly. 'Eve, dear, this gentleman's name is——'

'I'm already acquainted with Mr Gardener,' she cut in coolly, holding her hand out in a formal gesture of greeting. 'How nice to see you again, Mr Gardener,' she said with saccharine insincerity.

'Isn't it?' he returned mockingly, holding her hand a little longer than necessary, Eve thought. She winced slightly as he increased the pressure of that hand momentarily before releasing it with slow reluctance. 'Enjoying the sun?' he drawled, his gaze roaming over her with slow appreciation.

Eve stood as if turned to stone, remembering for the first time that she was only wearing the turquoise bikini she had been sunbathing in.

Normally it wouldn't have bothered her to greet people wearing so little, especially friends like Sophy and Patrick—and she still regarded the other woman as such, despite her recent interference. But Adam just made her feel conscious of her own near-nakedness—and his reaction to it.

His warmly caressing gaze made her feel hot all over. 'I'll just go and dress before lunch,' she said hastily.

'Please don't bother on my account,' Adam told her softly, his own clothing, although much more formal than her own, basically casual, the cream-coloured short-sleeved shirt revealing muscularly tanned arms covered in golden hair, beige-coloured trousers moulded to his narrow waist and thighs.

Eve gave him a warning look from beneath lowered lashes. In her seventies, her grandmother expected certain codes of behaviour from people, and simply wouldn't understand the way Adam behaved with Eve. *She* didn't understand it most of the time!

'We're only going to have a light meal served out here,' her grandmother told her innocently. 'No reason to change if you don't want to.'

'I want to,' Eve affirmed through gritted teeth. How she wanted to!

'I'll come in with you and take the luggage up to our rooms,' Patrick offered lightly.

'No, I'll do that,' Adam put in in measured tones. 'You stay and keep Sophy and Evelyn company; I'm sure the three of you must have a lot to talk about.'

Evelyn. Already Adam was on a first-name basis with her grandmother, and it had taken Paul, despite his father's almost lifetime association with the older woman, months, after he had taken over from his father, to pluck up the courage to call her Evelyn!

'If you're sure?' Patrick accepted amiably, already lowering his bulk down on to one of the loungers while Sophy poured them all a cool glass of lemonade, the matter of the luggage already decided as far as they were concerned.

Eve caught the look of coy satisfaction in Sophy's gleaming green eyes and turned angrily away, marching determinedly towards the house.

'Much as I like this tantalising view of your back——' Adam broke off the gentle mockery as Eve turned furiously, his hands raised defensively as her hands could be seen to be clenched at her sides. 'You didn't know I was coming here today, obviously,' he drawled drily.

'Obviously,' she bit out in controlled tones as she continued on into the house.

Adam caught up with her, keeping his strides measured to hers now that he had done so. 'I didn't plan this, you know,' he began coaxingly.

'No?' She turned to glare at him with eyes as turquoise as her bikini. 'You were no more Sophy and Patrick's "weekend guest" than I am.'

'That's where you're wrong.' He shook his head confidently. 'We were going to their cottage in the country...'

'I have news for you.' Eve gave him a pitying look. 'If indeed it is news,' she added suspiciously. 'Sophy and Patrick don't *have* a cottage in the country!'

'They don't?' Dark blond brows rose in what could only be genuine surprise.

'No!'

'Oh.' Adam was having trouble containing his humour now, running a hand over his mouth in an effort to control his show of mirth. But that couldn't erase the laughter from his eyes. 'What a pity Patrick met Sophy first; she's a woman after my own heart.' He sobered, his expression suddenly intense. 'If it had still been mine to give, of course,' he added softly.

Eve's mouth firmed. 'If you would like to bring the luggage up?'

She made no effort to help him carry the three suitcases up the wide staircase, knowing she was behaving childishly, but just so angry at the whole situation. Besides, a brief glance back showed her that he was managing the heavy cases with ease.

Going to Sophy and Patrick's 'cottage in the country', indeed! It didn't need two guesses—didn't need one *guess*—to know whose fabrication that had been; she was already certain.

And, as she had already known, Mrs Hodges had prepared the two best guest bedrooms, the lemon and cream for Sophy and Patrick, the blue and white for Adam.

Unfortunately, as Eve was all too well aware, the blue and white bedroom happened to be the one next to hers. But she couldn't possibly ask for that to be changed now, it would make herself too obvious to everyone. Not that she thought there was any possibility of Adam's attempting to enter her bedroom without permission—permission he would never get. No, the real problem—and what a problem it was—was that there was actually a bathroom connecting the two rooms, with a door going into each bathroom off it!

It hadn't always been this way. This was an old house, and the smaller room which was now a bathroom had once been another bedroom, for bathrooms had not been too plentiful when the house had originally been built. But that small room was a bathroom now, deliberately made that way so that the two bedrooms should appear to be a suite, a suite she and Adam Gardener were to share . . .

She couldn't help wishing that particular bathroom had never been put in!

'Comfortable bed.' Adam bent slightly and pressed down on the blue-covered mattress he would be using during his visit.

'The bathroom is through here.' Eve threw open the connecting door with a casualness she was far from feeling, promising herself she would remove all her personal toiletries from the room at the first opportunity. 'But I should knock first; I'm afraid you're sharing it.' She turned to leave.

'With you?'

She turned slowly at the door, knowing she had given herself away by her haste to be gone. 'As it happens, yes,' she bit out, looking at him challengingly, daring him to comment further.

He didn't, the single brow he raised eloquent enough.

Eve left him standing in the middle of the guest bedroom, closing her own door forcefully behind her a few seconds later, standing shakily just inside the room until she could breathe more easily.

The weekend promised to be a horrendous time for her. Her more unsuspecting grandmother could have no idea what she had done with her casual invitation...

'Where on earth do you think Sophy and Patrick found him?' Marina said speculatively, her dark blue eyes gleaming interestedly as she lay on Eve's bed later that evening.

These feminine confidences had become a ritual, first between two little girls, then two young women, and latterly between two fully grown women, although they hadn't been too regular in recent years.

But Eve had no doubts that Marina was going to totally explore this new interest she had in Adam Gardener as she settled more comfortably on the bed, her arms back behind her head as she let her thoughts drift.

Marina had only returned from her trip into town shortly after tea, Eve and her grandmother sharing a look of mutual horror at the number of shopping bags she had carried into the house, shopping she lost all interest in as soon as she was introduced to Adam Gardener. The sulky pout to her lush red-painted lips became a thing of the past as she instantly dazzled him with one of her warmer smiles, her hand resting intimately in his as she gazed up at him as if he were the only man in the world.

And, to Eve's disgust, Adam fell for it hook, line and sinker, as far as she could see!

And the two continued to monopolise each other until it was time to go and change for dinner—when it now seemed as if Eve had to *listen* to how attractive Marina found him!

'I don't think they "found" him anywhere,' she gently rebuked. 'He's a business acquaintance, and owns a gallery in New York, I believe,' she provided dismissively, wishing Marina would go to her own room so that she could finish getting ready. Paul would be arriving soon, and the last thing she wanted was him and Adam getting into conversation together. She would just have to hope that the dinner party the other evening stayed firmly out of the conversation over the weekend! What an idiot she had been to ever have lied in the first place.

'Rich, do you think?' Marina frowned consideringly.

'I *think* a person's wealth, or lack of it, shouldn't make any difference, if you like someone,' Eve reproved softly.

Marina grinned unabashed. 'I just happen to know I would be happier with a rich husband than with a poor one, regardless of whether or not I *like* him,' she mocked lightly.

Eve had given up being shocked by anything Marina said years ago, but even so...! 'Husband?' she repeated frowningly. 'You've only just met the man!'

'But I've been looking for a rich husband ever since I was seventeen,' Marina confided audaciously. 'I've just never met the right man yet. Adam Gardener could be him, don't you think?'

She *thought* Marina ought to have her head examined for even contemplating such a thing!

Regardless of the fact that Adam had been charming to Marina since they had first met, he *did* have the ability to totally demolish her if he chose. Brittle and selfish as Marina could sometimes appear, she didn't deserve to have less than a completely loving relationship with her husband.

And no, as far as Marina was concerned, she didn't believe she could have that with Adam Gardener.

'I don't believe it really matters what I think,' she answered drily, knowing that, no matter what anyone else's opinion might be, in the end Marina would only do what pleased her.

Marina grinned with anticipation, the bad-tempered shrew of the last few days completely erased. 'He really is an attractive individual.' She moved to the edge of the bed in preparation of leaving. 'Thank goodness I packed a couple of sexy dresses for the evenings—even if that was originally with the intention of tormenting old Paul!' she added with glee.

Eve shook her head ruefully. As far as she was aware, 'old Paul' never even noticed what Marina was wearing—unless it was to comment disparagingly on it! But then, that was probably what Marina had meant about 'tormenting' him.

'And I bought this fantastic dress today...' Marina murmured thoughtfully.

Eve was slightly suspicious of that reckless glint in Marina's eyes, but if she made a comment about this new dress Marina was sure to wear it anyway, so she might as well save her breath. 'Isn't it time you went and got ready?' she prompted, as Marina made no effort to get up off the bed now that she had sat up.

'In a minute.' Her cousin nodded absently. 'Lucky you.' She gave an exaggerated sigh. 'You actually get to share a bathroom with the man. Would you like to swap bedrooms for the weekend?' she asked brightly as the idea occurred to her.

'*I* might find the idea appealing.' Marina couldn't imagine just how much! 'But grandmother might raise a few objections.'

'Hm.' Marina gave a grimace, knowing that, for all that their grandmother was easy-going most of the time, when she chose to be firm about something she made sure no one was left in any doubts about it. 'Well, it was worth a try.' She shrugged. 'I have all evening and most of tomorrow to get to know Adam better, I suppose. See you later.' She smiled brightly, bouncing out of the room, her face alight with the new male interest in her life.

Eve ruefully moved across the room to close the bedroom door her cousin had left open, noticing as she did so the slight sound of movement behind her door that connected to the adjoining bathroom.

An image of a bare-chested Adam Gardener instantly sprang to mind, making her feel hot all over. Which was ridiculous; she had seen plenty of bare-chested men in her time, and none of them had affected her this way. *Including Paul*; the disloyal thought came into her mind unbidden. There was more to a relationship than sexual attraction, she told herself firmly. Much more.

Nevertheless, she could see that connecting bathroom they were to share was going to be a problem. It never had been before, but then, they didn't usually have anyone staying in that other bedroom. Sleeping-over guests were very rare at Ashton House. They didn't have that many guests at all, really, other than family and close friends.

Which reminded her of the fact that she had an even bigger problem than the connecting bathroom, where Adam Gardener was concerned!

Family and friends usually visited for the day or evening, which meant visitors had little reason to go up to the second floor of the house, let alone feel curious about what lay beyond the staircase that led to the third floor...

She already knew, from great personal experience, that one thing Adam Gardener didn't lack was curiosity. Or the ability to forcefully voice it!

CHAPTER FIVE

'Is the bedroom I'm using the one Paul sleeps in when he stays overnight?'

Eve spun round at the provocative question.

She and Adam were the only two down for dinner so far, Marina obviously making the most of the time to make herself as glamorous as possible, their grandmother was slower than she used to be, and goodness knew what was delaying Sophy and Patrick. Eve wished now she hadn't come downstairs so promptly.

She coolly met Adam's mocking gaze. 'Paul very rarely stays the night.'

'But when he does?' Adam persisted, just as attractive as the first time she had seen him, in a dark evening suit and snowy white shirt. If Marina had thought him handsome before, in the casual clothes of this afternoon, she was going to be bowled over when she saw him dressed like this!

As far as she could remember, there had never been occasion for Paul to need to stay the night here! 'I don't believe the sleeping arrangements of the man I intend to marry are any of your business,' she bit out tersely.

Adam's expression hardened, his eyes narrowed. 'They are if they include you.'

She drew in a sharp breath at the possessiveness in his voice. 'Adam——'

'Yes—Eve?' His gaze warmed caressingly as he stood much too close for comfort.

Eve swallowed hard, feeling herself grow warm all over at his proximity, moving sharply away as she felt herself falling under his spell. 'Marina might be more open to this type of seduction than I am.'

'How many times do I have to tell you this isn't a seduction?' Adam ground out harshly, the lazily charming man of the afternoon completely gone in his anger. 'Good heavens, woman, do I look the type of man to go around discussing marriage and children with every woman I meet?'

His eyes glowed almost gold in his anger, and Eve had the impression from the tight control he had over himself that it was an emotion he rarely allowed himself to be pushed to. But he couldn't be *serious*!

'Eve,' he took her unresisting hand and entwined his fingers with hers, 'we have to talk.' He shook his head impatiently. 'Properly, I mean, not just these tormenting conversations where I advance and you instantly retreat. But just believe this, I don't play games with other people's emotions. Or my own.'

Eve could hear the pain behind those last words, searching the hard face before her for some sign of what had caused that ache in his voice. It had been someone he loved that had hurt him, of course. But recently, or was it years ago? That deep curiosity she had mentally accused him of earlier surfaced within herself, and she knew a burning need to know more about this man, his past life, his family, his ...

'—lovely tonight, Evelyn,' Paul could be heard saying as he approached the drawing-room.

A moment of sheer panic possessed Eve. What was she doing, holding hands with Adam Gardener in this intimate way, on the verge of asking him to tell her about himself in a way he probably hadn't confided in anyone for years, if ever? Paul had arrived, the man she loved.

Regret registered in Adam's face before he slowly released her hand to slide his own into his trouser pocket, the two of them standing feet apart by the time Eve's grandmother and Paul entered the room together, her grandmother thanking him for the compliment he had just paid her.

Paul came to an abrupt halt, his face a picture of hostility as he recognised the man standing across the room.

'Darling, do you remember Mr Gardener?' Eve hastily moved to his side, putting her arm through the crook of his as he looked at her blankly. 'Grandmother invited Sophy and Patrick for the weekend, and Mr Gardener was their guest.'

That blank look disappeared from pale blue eyes, to be replaced by narrow-eyed speculation. 'Sophy and Patrick...' he murmured grimly, as if a number of questions had suddenly been answered. He eyed the other man coldly.

'We met once before,' Adam said smoothly as he held out the hand that wasn't in his pocket and forced Paul to acknowledge it unless he wanted to cause a scene in front of Eve's grandmother.

'Last weekend.' Paul nodded tersely after the briefest of handshakes. 'I seem to remember you were slightly—unwell.'

Eve saw Adam's mouth twitch at this Englishly polite way of saying he had appeared to be drunk. Unfortunately, Adam had none of that English reserve!

'I'd only had one glass of whisky,' he derided drily. 'It was the names that made me react in that way.' He shared a conspiratorial glance with Eve, causing her to look away awkwardly as Paul saw the exchange and glowered ominously.

'Names?' he prompted irritably.

'Of course, Paul.' Eve's grandmother smiled indulgently, completely unaware of the tension between the two men. 'Eve Eden and Adam Gardener!'

'Well, we all thought it was funny,' Adam murmured mockingly after several seconds when Paul remained straight-faced throughout.

'Very amusing,' Paul drawled, without the least sign of the emotion.

But, despite all that, Eve thought he was handling the situation very well, considering she hadn't been able to warn him of the other man's presence here; he hadn't been at home when she had telephoned him earlier.

As for the significance of the names, she knew that Paul believed the sooner her name became Lester, the better. She looked at him affectionately, as she too longed for that day.

But a sudden tingling sensation down her spine made her turn sharply towards Adam, swallowing hard at the fierce glow in his eyes. It was ridiculous to be made to feel guilty about smiling lovingly at the man she intended to marry...

'Now, isn't this cosy?' Sophy remarked as she and Patrick strolled into the room.

Poor Paul, Eve inwardly groaned, it really wasn't fair for him to be surrounded by all these people who took such delight in goading him!

But the chance for Sophy to do that any further at the moment was briefly taken out of her hands as their dinner party was made complete by Marina's entrance. And what an entrance it was!

Eve gasped out loud at the daring of the dark blue dress her cousin wore: strapless, the figure-hugging dress seemed to stay up by sheer willpower.

Their grandmother shared a pained look with Eve that seemed to say, It's no good criticising, because it will only cause a scene, and in the end Marina will only do what she wants to do.

But even for Marina the dress was outrageous, leaving all of them breathless with shock as she grinned triumphantly.

Adam was the first one to break the awkwardness of the moment, moving forward, smiling easily as he told Marina how stunning she looked.

Stunning wasn't quite the word Eve would have used herself, but she put her own feelings aside to try and soothe Paul's aghast reaction.

'It's only a family dinner party, for heaven's sake,' he muttered disgustedly.

She shrugged. 'Marina is attracted to Adam Gardener——'

'She's only known him a few hours,' he gasped. 'Hasn't she?' He frowned.

'Of course,' Eve dismissed. 'But you know Marina.'

'Too damned well,' he muttered. 'The man's too old for her.' He scowled at the other couple, in conversation a short distance away.

'Thirty-eight isn't old,' she heard herself defending, blushing deeply as Paul turned to her sharply. 'He happened to mention it earlier,' she excused lamely.

'I want you to stay away from him, Eve,' he bit out tersely as they all began to stroll through to dinner, Marina and her grandmother on either side of Adam Gardener, Sophy and Patrick just behind them. 'After all, what do we really know about the man?' Except that he was an acquaintance of Sophy and Patrick's, his tone seemed to say, and that was certainly no character reference in his eyes!

It had been destined to be a disaster of an evening; it always was when Adam Gardener was anywhere within the vicinity. And tonight was no exception.

If she were honest, she had to admit that most of it was Paul's own fault; his behaviour was childish, to say the least, as he deliberately set out to make the other man look small by conversing in a variety of subjects he believed Adam would have no knowledge of. But in that he had under-estimated the other man in a way Eve herself would never have done, even after so brief acquaintance as their first meeting. Adam was able to reply just as intelligently, so that in the end Paul was the one made to look small for behaving in such an obvious manner.

By the time the meal came to an end, Eve had a headache from all the tension, Paul was more dis-gruntled than ever, Marina thought Adam even more fascinating than before, Sophy watched them all with an air of triumphant satisfaction, while Patrick looked tolerantly amused, and her grand-mother looked at them all indulgently.

As a party of weekend guests, they were an ill-assorted lot!

After dinner wasn't much better, the two men getting into a very heated—on Paul's part at least, Adam managed to continue looking coolly unruffled—exchange on world politics.

But even so Eve could have wept with sheer frus-tration when Paul decided to leave shortly before eleven o'clock; he usually didn't leave until much later at the weekends.

'Do you have to go?' she sighed as she followed him out into the hallway.

'*Yes, I have to go,*' he bit out through gritted teeth, his expression relaxing slightly at her look of pained surprise at being shouted at by him in this way. 'I'm sorry,' he said tenderly, framing her heart-shaped face with his hands. 'But I can say, without a single doubt, that that was the worst evening I've spent in my entire life,' he added grimly.

Contrary to Paul, who still looked furiously angry, Eve was beginning to see the humour of it all now; if she didn't laugh, she would have to cry!

Paul scowled as she began to smile. 'I don't see anything in the least funny about all this.'

That was because he hadn't been sitting where she had all evening; it was the sort of evening that situation comedies were made of. But Paul's sense of humour seemed to be sadly lacking just recently, she realised with a frown.

'Perhaps you're right.' She sobered wearily. 'I'm sorry you've had such an awful time.'

'It isn't your fault,' he sighed. 'I can't imagine what Evelyn thought she was doing when she invited them all here.'

'She and Sophy have always been the best of friends,' Eve defended.

'I can't think why.' Paul didn't seem at all attuned to the fact that Eve was more than a little annoyed by his criticism of her grandmother.

After all, it was her grandmother's home, and she was perfectly entitled to invite into it whoever she chose. Paul had to be made to see that, as the two of them would be moving in here with her grandmother after their wedding in September.

'I don't think we really need to know why,' she rebuked gently. 'We just have to respect the fact that my grandmother has the right to choose her own friends.'

Paul didn't miss the underlying tension in her words this time. 'What's that supposed to mean?' he demanded indignantly.

Eve gave a weary sigh. 'Exactly what I said, that we have to respect——'

'I understood that part,' he cut in raspingly. 'I just don't understand the reason for the criticism. You can't actually be enjoying yourself with that ill-assorted crowd?' he challenged scornfully.

She didn't want to argue with him, for goodness' sake. 'Not particularly. But I do like Sophy and Patrick, and——'

'And Adam Gardener?' His eyes were narrowed. 'Do you "like" him, too?'

She gasped at the way he made the question sound like an insult, stepping back slightly. 'Paul!' she cried in rebuke.

He scowled unrepentantly. 'Well, you seem to have been spending a lot of time with him.'

'What on earth do you mean?' she said indignantly, paling slightly as she imagined him somehow having found out about her deception concerning the dinner party. Oh, how she wished she had never told that lie. It certainly hadn't been worth the worry it had caused her since that night!

Paul glowered angrily. 'Every time I turn around lately, I fall over the damned man. And always with you, it seems,' he added, glaring at her.

Her breath left her body in a relieved sigh at his continued unawareness of her omission concerning the dinner party the other evening; she was sure he would have mentioned it by now if he had known of it. 'When first we practise to deceive...' But she hadn't set out to deceive, merely avoid a confrontation—like the one they were having right now.

'I've explained about the party last weekend,' she told him agitatedly. 'And if you hadn't left me alone so long while you went off talking to other people, he wouldn't have been able to——' She broke off abruptly, aghast at what she had just said.

Paul was obviously stunned by the outburst, too. 'What on earth has got into you? I've never heard you talk like that before.' He shook his head, frowning with dark disapproval.

Neither had she, it was completely unlike her. *But long overdue,* a voice of mischief said in her head. What on earth *had* got into her?

'I can see that further conversation between the two of us tonight is a waste of time,' Paul bit out coldly at her lack of response. 'I'll call you tomorrow, and maybe then you'll be in a more—reasonable frame of mind.' His tone implied that he sincerely hoped that would be the case.

'But, Paul——'

'Goodnight, Eve,' he said icily, ignoring her imploringly outstretched hand, striding across the entrance hall to close the huge oak door behind him with a decisive slam.

Nothing like that had ever happened between them before; she and Paul never argued. Never. But they certainly had just now, she acknowledged dazedly.

She just stood there in the cavernous hallway, a lonely figure. And at that moment she did feel very alone.

'The course of true love not running smoothly again?' mocked a voice that was fast becoming her own personal torment.

Eve turned around slowly. 'Don't you have anything better to do than spy on me?'

One brow raised questioningly at her lack of anger. 'I wasn't spying on you,' he said softly. 'I was on my way to bed.'

Eve frowned. 'Why?'

He shrugged. 'There didn't seem anything to stay up for.'

Her eyes widened. 'But you and Marina were getting on so well...'

'I'm not even going to acknowledge the stupidity of that remark by answering it,' Adam rasped disparagingly. 'Did you and Paul have an argument?'

She stiffened defensively. 'Why on earth should you think that?'

He gave another shrug. 'The speed with which he appears to have left.'

She gave an exasperated sigh. 'We left the drawing-room over fifteen minutes ago.'

'I know exactly how long ago it was,' he drawled, his gaze softening, becoming sensual. 'If I had been the one saying goodnight to you, I wouldn't have left until morning.'

He said the most outrageous things... But oh, what a picture of heady delight his words evoked.

Everything about this man exuded sensuality, and his complete confidence in his ability to keep the lady of his choice happy in his arms. Unfortunately, Eve seemed to be that lady at that moment!

'You *are* the one saying goodnight to me, Mr Gardener,' she pointed out coldly. 'And even if you have the wish to remain standing in the hallway all night, I certainly don't!' She turned on her heel and began walking up the wide staircase.

Adam caught up with her after she had taken only a few steps, grasping her arm to turn her to face him. Eve was totally disconcerted as she found herself on eye-level with him as he stood a couple of steps down from her, mesmerised by the gold flecks she could see in the darkness of his eyes as they stood closer than they ever had before.

'I don't want to stand in a hallway all night, Eve,' he grated with soft intensity. 'Elegant as this one is. I want to be with you, make love with you, lie with you until morning comes. I *ache* with wanting that!'

Eve felt a quivering heat down her spine at his evocative words.

'But no matter what you think of me,' he ground out harshly, a nerve pulsing in his cheek, 'I wouldn't even attempt to make that longing a fact while you're still deceiving Paul Lester into thinking you're going to marry him.'

Eve gasped, as much at his apparent anger with *her* as with what he was actually saying. 'I'm not deceiving Paul,' she defended breathlessly when she found her voice again.

'You're deceiving everyone—but most of all yourself.' Adam shook his head dismissively. 'You're in love with love, not Paul. But until you can see that, I can't do a damned thing to change the situation.'

There could be no doubting his anger with her now, and Eve bristled indignantly. 'This so-called morality doesn't seem to stop you having conversations like this one!'

His fingers tightened on her arm. 'It's my "morality", as you call it,' he bit out, 'that stops me from taking you up those stairs and *showing* you the truth of what I'm saying!' His eyes glittered furiously.

'There's nothing wrong with your ego, is there?' she scorned.

'It isn't my damned ego talking, for heaven's sake,' he rasped impatiently.

'Stop swearing.' She frowned at his vehemence.

'*Stop changing the subject,*' Adam returned forcefully.

'I'm not changing the subject, I'm *ending* it.' She moved abruptly away from him, looking at him with wide eyes for several seconds before turning and running up the stairs.

There was only one place for her to go, the one place she had to go, and she ran to her studio as if it were a refuge.

Tears squeezed between her tightly closed lids as she stood in the centre of the room, feeling totally desolate. Her whole world seemed to have been put into a turmoil. She and Paul had argued, something unheard of before. And, much as she wished it weren't true, she knew that most of the reason for that had been because parts of her conversations with Adam kept coming into her mind at the most inopportune times, fuelling the tension between Paul and herself.

She would have to telephone Paul in the morning and apologise, of course—that last outburst of hers had been entirely unwarranted. If she hadn't told that ridiculous lie about Sophy and Patrick's dinner guest in the first place, then she probably wouldn't have been feeling so agitated and retaliated the way she had. She just hadn't expected that either Paul or herself would ever see Adam Gardener again.

But it was no good finding excuses; she and Paul were at odds with each other, and it was a feeling that made her feel very uneasy within herself, as if the very foundations of her carefully planned life were being rocked.

She had loved Paul from a distance ever since she could remember, although he hadn't really seemed to notice her in return until he had taken

over the practice after his father's death two years
ago. But even then he had kept a businesslike distance, and it had only been recently, the last year
or so, that they had started to become close.

Why, oh, why had Adam Gardener had to come
into her life now? Another couple of months and
she and Paul would have been married. Knowing
what a healthy respect Adam had for marriage, she
felt sure he wouldn't have even tried to get close to
her then, no matter what his own feelings might
have been. As it stood now, with her neither free
nor officially out of his reach, he wouldn't leave
her in peace.

As for the weekend, she still had the rest of that
to get through!

It was a strange sensation, not unlike floating, and
yet she knew there was no danger of her falling,
could feel herself being held and supported as if
she were as light as gossamer.

She liked the feeling, snuggling down more
comfortably into that cosy warmth.

And then she wasn't floating any more, but lying
on soft down, sinking, sinking, cocooned in its
fluffy warmth. It was the most wonderful sensation she had ever...

'Oh, no, you don't, Sleepyhead,' cajoled an
amused voice as the cocoon was gently taken from
her. 'No, Eve.' A throaty chuckle accompanied this
second reproof as she tried to pull back the soft
warmth. 'You can't go to bed in your dress.'

Suddenly the return of the cocoon didn't seem half so important, her eyes opening wide as she became aware of the fact that it had been the duvet on her bed she had been trying to wrap around herself.

She stared straight up into Adam Gardener's tenderly amused face.

'I thought that might manage to get your attention,' he drawled softly, sitting on the side of the bed as he looked down at her with caressing brown eyes.

She swallowed hard, too wary of his close proximity to risk moving herself. 'What time is it?' From the quietness in the house, she knew it had to be late.

'After one,' Adam confirmed huskily, his face all angles in the golden glow given off from the bedside lamp. 'You must have been really tired, to have fallen asleep like that. I brought you here and you didn't even wake!'

Emotionally exhausted. Arguing with Paul had upset her badly, and she had cried herself to sleep.

'Obviously you weren't?' she said questioningly, his dinner jacket and bow-tie having been discarded since Eve had seen him earlier, the snowy white shirt partly unbuttoned down his chest, dark gold hair glinting in that open V; but he gave little appearance of having actually gone to bed as he had said he was earlier.

He smoothed her hair back from her brow with gentle fingers. 'We'll talk about what I was or wasn't in the morning. Right now, I think we should get you out of your clothes so that you can go back to sleep.'

'I can do it,' she told him with alarm, instinctively clutching her dress to her.

Adam gave a rueful smile. 'I had a feeling you might say that.' He stood up slowly to look down at her. 'And I'm sure you can do it—if you don't fall asleep again first,' he chided indulgently as her lids began to flutter closed.

Her eyes weren't closing because she was tired, but because his being here in her bedroom, his shirt partly unbuttoned to reveal the hard strength of his chest, was having the strangest effect on her.

But she could still see him, even with her eyes closed, every masculine inch of him.

'I wasn't going to do this. I promised myself I wouldn't,' Eve suddenly heard him groan. 'But I can't help myself!'

She had known what he couldn't stop himself doing even before his arms gathered her up against him and his mouth claimed hers hardily. It had been inevitable since the moment she'd woken up to look into his tenderly amused face. Something had happened inside her at that moment, something too fleeting to define, and yet she couldn't deny that it had happened, or that it had happened before too.

Like thirsty travellers in a desert they drank from each other's lips, sipping, tasting, until passion flared and they were no longer content to sip, drinking deeply, their mouths moving together hungrily.

Adam's skin felt firm and hard beneath her touch, his muscles rippling convulsively as she unbuttoned his shirt to know him fully, tempted by that silken flesh, her lips lowering to taste him.

His gasp of pleasure gave her a heady sense of gladness that she had dared to touch him in this way, and she felt the tension of his body beneath her.

Heated lips nibbled against her throat, trailing fire, and it was her turn to gasp out loud as those lips moved moistly to capture the tip of her breast through the thin material of her dress.

She shivered with delight at that gentle tugging on her flesh, her back arched as pleasure flooded warmly through her, her nipple hard and pulsing against him.

She closed her eyes expectantly as Adam laid her gently back against the pillows, his lips moving in a featherlike touch from her mouth to the tip of her nose, softly kissing her closed lids before standing up.

Eve was quivering with tension, waiting for him to rejoin her.

'Goodnight, my darling.' His voice came, not from beside her as she had expected, but from across the room. 'My elusive Unicorn,' he added huskily.

Her lids flew wide open in alarm but, in the brief moment it took her to turn to him, the door was softly closing as he left her bedroom.

The Unicorn!

Good lord, why hadn't she realised long before now that, after finding her in her studio, Adam would now know exactly who The Unicorn was?

CHAPTER SIX

'HE'S ecstatic about the way things have worked out,' Sophy told her enthusiastically the next morning, after bursting into Eve's bedroom unannounced shortly after nine o'clock.

Which was certainly more than Eve was! She had a feeling Adam wasn't going to give her any peace at all now that he had discovered the true identity of The Unicorn.

Why did she have to go and fall asleep in her studio? Why did Adam have to come looking for her? And *find* her!

She had slept very badly after he'd left her room the night before, wanting to go and tell him right then and there not to get any clever ideas concerning her just because he now knew she was the artist he had been searching for. And that applied to Sophy, too, now that her secret was out!

Eve continued to brush her hair dry in front of the mirror on her dressing-table, having just washed it beneath the shower's spray. '*Things* haven't worked out at all,' she snapped, her face very pale, her eyes appearing deeply turquoise against that paleness.

'But——'

'Who or what I am doesn't make the slightest difference to the way *I* feel about Adam Gardener,' she firmly cut across Sophy's protest.

The other woman's gaze narrowed on her speculatively. 'And how do you feel about him?'

She replaced the brush carefully on the dressing-table in front of her, her hand shaking slightly. 'I think,' she said slowly, 'that he's a very dangerous man.'

'Dangerous?' Sophy gave a puzzled frown, for once disconcerted. 'But he isn't in the least—— Or do you mean he's dangerous to the life you've chosen for yourself?' She brightened at the idea.

That was exactly what Eve meant. Adam had come along and upset it all.

'I just mean dangerous,' she repeated flatly. 'Shall we go downstairs now?' She stood up with finality. 'I have a terrible headache, and I would like to take something for it.'

Sophy made no effort to follow her across the room. 'You're in a very strange mood today.' She was frowning again.

'I told you,' Eve shrugged dismissively, 'I have a headache.'

'It isn't only that.' Sophy shook her head, her gaze searching the closed expression on Eve's face. 'You seem somehow—different.'

Different. Was it really that obvious for anyone to see just by looking at her?

'I'm not different,' she said dully.

'Eve——'

'I'm late for breakfast already,' she concluded abruptly, leaving the room, as Sophy was making no effort to do so.

'Eve, if I've been too pushy——' Sophy broke off at Eve's side as she rounded on her with incredulous eyes. 'OK,' she shrugged with a pained grimace, 'I *know* I've been pushy. But——'

'It's for my own good—right?' Eve finished with bitterness. 'The fact that Paul isn't always co-operative with the plans you outline has nothing whatsoever to do with it?'

The other woman frowned at the scornful outburst. 'Eve...?'

She gave a harsh laugh, shaking her head. '"The worm has turned"?'

'That term hardly applies to you,' Sophy said in an injured voice, the two of them clattering down the stairs in high heels.

'I'm not a child who needs her life organised for her, either!' Her face was flushed with anger.

'I wasn't trying to—— Well, perhaps I was,' Sophy conceded at her reproving look. 'But Adam is a fascinating man, and...'

'And you knew right from the beginning of your machinations that I was going to marry Paul,' she bit out tautly. 'Oh, never mind, Sophy,' she dismissed impatiently at the other woman's hurt expression. 'Let's just forget the whole subject.'

Was going to marry Paul; the words kept reverberating around in her mind, although Sophy didn't seem to have noticed that past tense in her statement. Because that was what it was for now. She couldn't, in all honesty, marry Paul at a time when Adam Gardener seemed able to take her in his arms and elicit a response from her any time he chose to do so. Paul deserved more from her than that.

That had been the reason she was unable to sleep after Adam had left her; she had been trying to decide what to do, knowing there was really only one thing she could do. And that was to tell Paul she couldn't go through with the wedding until she was over this madness. If he still wanted her then...

'*What?*'

She could understand Paul's anger and pain at what she had had to tell him, she knew the same emotions herself. But what else could she do?

'It's just for now, Paul,' she attempted to placate him.

'You want to call off our wedding plans because of some juvenile interest you feel for a man who is completely unsuitable——'

'If it were a juvenile interest, Paul, then it wouldn't be of any importance.' The way she reacted to Adam was far from juvenile. That was what frightened her.

She had excused herself from the breakfast table after drinking a hurried cup of coffee, leaving a puzzled Sophy watching her departure; she had been anxious to get away from Ashton House before she had to see Adam, Mrs Hodges having informed

her when she arrived downstairs that he and Patrick
had gone out riding.

On the drive over to Paul's apartment she had
gone over and over again in her mind what she had
to say to him, and not once had it got any easier.

His reaction had been expected, and just as dis-
tressing as she had known it would be.

She had told him everything, sparing herself
nothing, even telling him about the dinner party he
had been unable to attend when Adam had been
the other guest there, and not the female friend of
Sophy and Patrick's that she had claimed it to be.
Paul had been dumbfounded at her deception, but
even so, none of it seemed to have prepared him
for the announcement she had just made about not
being able to marry him with her emotions as confused as they were.

'You're over-reacting——'

'But surely you can see,' she looked at him
pleadingly, tears balanced on her lashes, 'that it
wouldn't be fair to you to go through with the
wedding when another man can cause such a response in me?' Her cheeks were fiery red at the
admission, still slightly shocked herself at that
response.

Paul's face darkened with anger. 'I can see that
you're allowing your pre-wedding nerves to let you
imagine this physical attraction—which is all it can
possibly be,' he dismissed scathingly, 'is more important than years of knowing each other, caring
for each other. Gardener is nothing but a phony

sun-tan and a smooth charm!' he rasped disgustedly.

There was nothing in the least 'phony' about Adam, nor 'smooth', for that matter, and she and Paul both knew it. But she could appreciate that jealous anger was making Paul say these things.

'I can also see Sophy O'Donnell's interfering hand behind this!' His eyes glittered furiously at the thought.

Eve sighed. 'Sophy only introduced the two of us; she couldn't force my reaction to him.'

Paul gave a disparaging snort. 'A man like that would take delight in deliberately causing friction between us just because we were doing the decent thing by getting married!'

Again he spoke out of jealousy and not truth. If Adam had only been out to cause trouble between them, was really the selfish type of man Paul was claiming him to be, then he would have made love to her the night before, not left her as he had. Because she certainly wouldn't have been able to say no...

But he hadn't done that, and she knew it had been because of that 'moral code' she had taunted him about, not because he had found any resistance on her part.

'Why else do you think a man of his age has remained single,' Paul stormed, 'if not because he would rather have his fun with someone else's woman?'

That was just it, she was no longer anyone's woman. She couldn't marry Paul feeling as she did about Adam, and yet she knew she wasn't in love with Adam. She loved Paul, had always loved Paul—she just couldn't help kissing Adam back whenever he chose to take her into his arms!

'I don't think that's the reason he's never married, Paul,' she began slowly.

'What would you know about it?' he scoffed, his eyes silver with anger. 'You've never met anyone like him before, and you're completely out of your depth with that brand of sophisticated excitement. What on earth am I saying?' he groaned, his eyes closed in disbelief.

'Exactly the same things I have for the last half an hour.' She gave a sad smile at the acknowledgement. 'And I couldn't, in all conscience, marry you with that between us.'

He scowled darkly. 'Surely I'm the one it affects the most, and if I'm sure it's just a temporary aberration...'

'But we don't know that, Paul, and so I can't do that to you.' She shook her head in firm denial. 'I think you've taken this all wonderfully.' She touched his arm gently. 'I just don't know what happened...' Her eyes were shadowed with pain.

'I do.' He was breathing heavily in his agitation. 'I've been too much the gentleman, that's the trouble. Maybe if I had made love to you instead of holding back until after we were married, none of this would have happened. I just wanted to treat

you with respect and—and love. But what do I have
to lose now...'

Eve didn't even attempt to fight him as he took
her fiercely into his arms and began to kiss her with
hard lips; she owed him this much at least.

Usually she found enjoyment in Paul's arms, felt
cherished by his kisses, but this morning he was
angry, so angry. And her lack of response just
seemed to make him angrier, so much so that Eve
suddenly became shakingly aware of how alone they
were in his apartment. And anger was apt to make
people do the strangest things, things normally out
of character. Not this way, it couldn't be this way!

She wrenched her mouth free of his. 'Paul, stop
this!' she gasped, genuinely frightened, for both of
them. 'You're only making the situation worse...'

His mouth twisted, as swollen as Eve's felt beneath the tentative touch of her tongue. 'How could
it possibly be worse than it already is?' he said bitterly, not relinquishing his hold on her in the
slightest. 'Your becoming involved with Adam
Gardener has destroyed all our plans.' He scowled.

'But surely you can see——'

'All I can see clearly is that you no longer intend
to marry me.' He put her abruptly away from him,
as if suddenly aware of the way he had been holding
her against her will, thrusting his hands into his
trouser pockets and stepping back.

Eve looked at him pleadingly once again. 'It's
only until I've sorted out my emotions.'

His mouth twisted. 'I wonder how many other poor fools have heard the same thing and gone on hoping?'

She frowned. 'But it really is only until I feel more sure of myself.'

He glared, his mouth thinning. 'And how long do you expect that to take?'

His scepticism was so obvious, and it didn't help that Eve knew she had no real answer for him.

'I don't know...' She gave a self-conscious grimace, feeling very uncomfortable, wringing her hands together nervously.

'I do,' Paul bit out tautly. 'You'll never marry me now.'

'That's not true,' she cried, desperate at the thought of losing him. 'Things just have to be delayed for a while,' she insisted.

'Indefinitely was the way you put it a few minutes ago, I believe,' he reminded bitterly.

What else could she say? She didn't *want* to cancel her wedding to Paul, it had been her dream for as long as she could remember, but no woman should marry one man while desiring another.

There was something else she had come to terms with during her wakeful hours of the night; she did desire Adam, would gladly have given herself to him the night before. And *that* was the reason she couldn't go through with marrying Paul, not until she was sure the attraction she felt towards Adam wasn't a temptation she would give in to, married to Paul or not.

'Until I'm doing the right thing for both of us,' she nodded.

Paul turned away disgustedly. 'And to think I believed you had come here today to apologise for your outburst to me last night,' he muttered with self-derision.

'But don't you realise,' she looked at him imploringly, 'that my outburst of last night is all part of what's been happening to me over the last week?'

Paul frowned heavily. 'I don't think I care for the changes,' he rasped dully.

She *was* changing, Eve acknowledged sadly on the drive back to Ashton House, and, like Paul, she wasn't sure those changes were for the better. But, until she could be sure she had stopped changing, it wouldn't be fair to even try and commit herself to marrying Paul. He might not even like her at the end of all this!

She wasn't altogether sure she liked herself at the moment, after what she had just had to do!

Not in the mood to face anyone, she quickly made her way up to her studio once she got back to the house. Time enough later to explain—at least, partially—that her wedding to Paul was off for the moment. And, taking into account the fact that Paul hadn't seemed eager to see her again, she didn't know if the wedding would ever be on again!

The studio was full of paintings she already had finished for the winter exhibition, images that were so much a part of her, resting against all of the walls.

Ironically there was nothing now standing in the way of telling Sophy to go ahead with the exhibition as she had planned; she doubted Paul cared any more what she did.

She walked despondently about the studio, gently touching a canvas here, gazing unseeingly at another canvas there.

In the past she had always found pleasure in her work; today she couldn't find pleasure in anything, and her life seemed in a shambles.

She had little enthusiasm for the canvases she had yet to finish, either, making her wonder if there *could* be a winter exhibition, after all.

'Your grandmother said you were back; I had a feeling you might be up here.'

Eve spun around like a startled doe at the sound of Adam's voice behind her, eyeing him warily as he stood in the doorway at the top of the stairs.

'May I?' He indicated his desire to enter the studio as she made no effort to answer him.

She swallowed hard, finding difficulty in breathing, this the first time she had seen him since she had lain so wantonly in his arms the night before.

'It looks as if you already have.' Her reply was sharper than she would have wished, but then, Adam shouldn't have invaded her privacy—especially when she was feeling so rawly vulnerable!

He held up his hands placatingly. 'If you would rather I went away again...'

She would rather the *whole world* went away until she felt more able to face it; most of all she would rather not be anywhere near the man who had been instrumental in starting the tumbling down of the life she had planned for herself.

'No, come in,' she heard herself say dully. 'After all, it won't be the first time you've been up here, will it?' she dismissed harshly.

Adam stepped frowningly into the studio, his hands thrust into the pockets of the black trousers he wore, the cuffs turned back to just below the elbows on his pale blue shirt.

Eve could feel an involuntary tightening of her defences, as if her body was more than usually aware of the danger this man was to her. He had no right to affect her this way!

'I didn't mean to intrude last night,' he told her softly, his dark gaze compelling. 'It was just that I was worried when you didn't come back to your room, and decided to come looking for you.'

'And in your search you stumbled across The Unicorn,' she said derisively.

'I found *you*,' he corrected evenly, his dark gaze still holding hers captive.

Her head went back challengingly. 'The Unicorn,' she repeated firmly.

'I wanted you in my life long before I knew anything about that.' He stood in front of her now, so close that the warmth of his breath stirred the soft wisps of her fringe.

'Did you?' Her throat ached with the effort of holding back unshed tears.

Adam looked down at her searchingly. 'Eve, where have you been all morning?'

Her throat moved convulsively, but still she held her emotions in check. 'I went to tell the man I've loved all my life that I can't marry him, because of my response to a man I've just met,' she told him in a clear voice, only a slight underlying tremor to give away her true feelings.

Adam breathed in harshly before breathing out again in a low sigh. 'That must have been very difficult for you to do.'

If he had been gloatingly pleased, looked in the least triumphant, showed even the slightest pleasure in the act that had caused her so much pain, Eve might have managed to remain in control. As it was, his understanding of the trauma she had been through knocked down the walls of her defences and opened up the floodgates.

She literally fell into his arms, her body shaking with sobs, seeking comfort and reassurance, receiving it unquestioningly; Adam murmured soothingly into her hair, one hand moving comfortingly up and down her spine as he held her lightly to him.

The loud hiccup she gave in the midst of the tears broke the tension, and she gave a watery smile in return as Adam smiled down at her affectionately at her self-conscious grimace.

'Not exactly elegant,' she sighed, wiping away the tears with her fingertips, knowing her cheeks would be flushed, her nose bright red.

'It's only movie stars who manage to cry and still look beautiful,' he said drily. 'And that's only because for the most part, they're paid small fortunes to look that way!'

No surer way than that of telling her cheeks *were* flushed, and her nose *was* bright red! Oh, well, she had asked for it.

'I'm sorry about that,' she grimaced, her movements awkward in her embarrassment.

'I would say it was long overdue.' Adam gently smoothed back the softness of her hair from her face. 'Paul didn't take the news well?' he prompted softly.

She gave a harsh laugh at the understatement. 'What do you think?'

'I think he probably said a lot of things he now regrets,' Adam said with a sigh.

Eve drew in a ragged breath. 'I doubt that very much. All that he said was the truth.'

Adam looked as if he doubted that. 'But for all the shouting, I take it he still wanted to marry you?'

'And why would you "take" that?' she shot back defensively, looking for criticism.

He shrugged. 'Did he?'

'I don't think——'

'Surely I have a right to know? After all, I am the other man.'

'You aren't the "other man",' she flared indignantly. 'There isn't *another* man, just me having pre-wedding nerves that I thought it best to resolve before we go through the big step of getting married.'

Adam looked at her chidingly. 'That wasn't the impression you gave a few minutes ago.'

Her cheeks were flushed. 'I might have known you would throw that back at me.'

'I have a feeling you're spoiling for a fight,' he drawled drily. 'But I'm not going to oblige you.' He shook his head.

'You aren't?' she said with unconcealed sarcasm.

'No. Not for the reasons you want, anyway,' he added chidingly. 'I still can't get over the fact that I had The Unicorn in front of me all the time and just didn't know it. And no, that has nothing to do with the way I feel about you,' he derided as her mouth thinned. 'I'm amazed *you're* The Unicorn, overjoyed. But I'm also mad as hell at you.' He sobered, frowning darkly.

'At me?' she gasped.

'Of course at you,' he confirmed impatiently.

'But why?' she frowned.

'Because you've successfully hidden yourself away from the world all these years.' He shook his head in puzzlement.

Her head went back. 'I haven't hidden away from anyone.'

'Then what have you been doing?'

'I've been busy working,' she defended.

'But no one knows your identity except a few close friends and family,' he pointed out softly.

'That doesn't make any difference to my work,' she instantly retorted.

He strolled across the room to stand in front of one of the finished but so far 'unshown' canvases, gazing at it with obvious enjoyment. 'No, it doesn't make any difference to the brilliance of your work,' Adam acknowledged huskily.

The painting was of miles and miles of seemingly endless golden corn waving gently in the breeze, so lifelike that there was vibrancy in every brush-stroke. And in the centre of that golden beauty was a little girl carrying a bunch of buttercups in her tiny hands.

Adam's hand moved out to the canvas, almost touching it but not quite. 'She looks very much like you must have done as a child.' He smiled gently. 'Like the little girl *we* might have one day.'

She stiffened. 'We aren't having a little girl.'

'No, I suppose they could both be boys,' he acknowledged with a nod. 'That was why I said she looked like the little girl we *might* have.'

Eve strode forcefully across the room to his side, looking up at him angrily. 'The fact that I have—temporarily—called off my wedding to Paul does not mean that I intend becoming involved with you.'

'You may not intend it,' he grasped her arms, his gaze warm, 'but it is going to happen. Remember, I said the only thing holding me back was your commitment to Paul. Now that no longer exists——'

'Temporarily,' she reminded forcefully.

'Whatever.' He smiled dismissively, framing her face with his big hands before lowering his head to take her mouth in a slow, lingering kiss.

By the time he raised his head to look down at her, Eve had no will of her own, speech was her only defence. 'But I don't love you,' she told him desperately, achingly. 'I love Paul.'

'You're attracted enough to me to realise you can't marry him because of it.' Adam's eyes had darkened with grim determination. 'And now the barrier of your impending wedding has gone, I intend to show you how good it's going to be between us. No holds barred!'

She swallowed hard at the purposeful expression on his face. 'But——'

'No holds barred, Eve,' he warned softly, before leaving as quietly as he had arrived.

No holds barred, he had said. Eve couldn't help the feelings of panic those words evoked. What had his behaviour been before, if not 'no holds barred'?

CHAPTER SEVEN

'SO WHEN I left college I——' Adam tilted his head back to quirk one eyebrow at her. 'Am I boring you?'

This would teach her to claim she knew nothing about him!

She had been trying to get back into her work all afternoon, having decided while she picked at the food on her plate during lunch that the best way to block out the shambles of her life for a few hours was to try and work: when she painted, she didn't think of anything other than what she was working on.

Unfortunately, Adam had decided that the two of them should spend the afternoon together. And, much as she tried, Eve couldn't get him to leave the studio. Short of carrying him out of course, which, considering their difference in sizes, was an impossibility!

And so she was stuck with him, lying all over her couch as he told her his life story from the moment he had his untimely entrance into the world in the middle of a department store while his mother was out shopping, through his very happy childhood as the only child of very doting parents, to his school years, and then on to his time spent at college. And it had all been told with such an air of self-mockery that Eve couldn't help being amused—and intrigued.

She had also spent the last half-hour *not* working on her most recent canvas, but on a charcoal sketch of the man himself. He was an artist's dream; his bone structure and skin tone just cried out to be put on canvas. In fact—he was gorgeous!

'No, you aren't boring me,' she assured him, her voice husky.

'Good.' He grinned, settling himself down comfortably on the sofa again. 'I'm just getting to the good bit.'

She had already guessed that, realising that his life had really only just begun when he had acquired the qualifications he had wanted and left college to branch out into business for himself.

He made light of those early achievements, and yet Eve could guess at the real truth behind them, and the sprinkling of silver among the dark blond hair told its own story.

'Women,' he announced starkly.

Eve looked at him sharply, startled briefly. 'What about them?'

He shrugged. 'There haven't been any for some time,' he instantly dismissed. 'I had the usual wild youth, but maturity brings with it a certain morality. I have lots of friends in the States, of both sexes, and there was once someone I cared for, but somehow it just never worked out. Now I know the reason why.'

'Oh?' she said lightly, although she had a feeling she knew what was coming next.

'Hm—you were still playing with your dolls when I started wondering about a wife!'

Not exactly the answer she had expected—but it was close enough!

'You don't really believe that for every person there is only one other person in the world who can be completely compatible to them?' She carried on sketching as she waited for his answer.

Adam gave her question more consideration than she thought it merited; she had meant the remark mockingly. But the longer he took to make a reply, the more her curiosity burned to hear his answer!

'One perfect person, yes.' He finally nodded. 'But dozens of other people that you could find happiness with, lasting happiness.'

'And the chances of finding that "one perfect person"?' She had given up all pretence of working now, this conversation intriguing her.

'Remote,' he conceded drily. 'Although with travel made easier it's not as remote as it once must have been. And we were destined not to miss each other,' he added smugly.

She had been wondering when he would turn the conversation on to a personal level. But her own curiosity had got the better of her for the moment. 'Oh—why?' she prompted lightly.

He quirked his brows. 'Isn't that obvious—Eve?'

She sighed. 'Our names don't——'

'Not just the names, Eve.' He shook his head slowly as he stood up. 'There are too many other coincidences,' he continued as he walked towards her. 'There's the fact that I fell in love with The Unicorn's work long before I met you, the fact that I decided to come over here in search of the artist at this particular time. A few months later and I would have been too late,' he rasped tautly, his hands moving up to gently cup either side of her face. 'I can't tell you how glad I am that didn't happen,' he murmured softly as his head lowered to hers. 'So very glad, Eve.'

At that moment so was she, seduced by him once again, loving the feel of his mouth against hers. He nibbled softly and then feasted on her lips, one moment tormenting her with the gentle nip of his teeth, the next moment possessing her with velvety gentleness.

'We were made for each other, Eve,' Adam groaned against her. 'Made to love like this, to lie in each other's arms——'

'Like hell you were!'

Adam was wrenched abruptly away from her, and then followed the loud cracking of knuckles against hard flesh.

It was all happening too quickly for Eve to be able to take in what was going on, her senses still whirling from Adam's kisses.

By the time she had recovered enough to realise Paul had been the one to burst into her studio and cause all the mayhem, Adam was lying amongst several of her canvases that lay propped against the wall, where Paul had knocked him.

She couldn't believe this was happening; she'd had no warning, too enrapt in Adam's lovemaking to be conscious of anything else.

Her eyes widened with renewed horror as she saw what was about to happen next, Adam's face full of glowering anger as he rose slowly to his feet, his gaze fixed belligerently on Paul as he gingerly rubbed his jaw where it had taken the full force of the other man's painful blow.

Paul stood across the room from him, breathing hard, a look of satisfaction on his face.

'Adam, no!' Eve cried desperately as he made a lunge towards the other man, his intent obvious. 'Please,' she added achingly as he turned to her frowningly.

He drew in a ragged breath, nodding slowly, reluctantly. 'This isn't the place for this,' he conceded, his jaw obviously paining him as he worked it slowly round to feel the damage that had been done. 'The work in here is priceless——'

'I wasn't thinking about the paintings,' she protested impatiently. 'The two of you fighting isn't going to solve anything.'

She still had trouble coming to terms with the fact that Paul had burst in here and behaved in this way. He had been angry earlier, yes, but before she had left his flat she had believed he had understood, if not completely accepted, what she had tried to explain to him. And how true had her fears concerning her weakness to Adam been; only a few hours later and Paul had found her in the other man's arms!

'Hitting him made me feel a hell of a lot better,' Paul ground out with a scornful glance at the other man.

'That form of backstabbing would appeal to a man like you,' Adam returned scathingly.

Adam's derision might be justified, Eve accepted; after all, Paul had taken him completely unawares. But the two of them acting like schoolchildren wasn't going to help the situation at all.

'Please.' She sighed wearily. 'Paul, why are you here?' She frowned.

His jaw tightened. 'Well, certainly not to walk in and see you in *his* arms!'

'Then maybe you shouldn't have just "walked" in,' Adam rasped as Eve blushed uncomfortably at the accusation in Paul's tone.

Paul's eyes gleamed palely as he looked at the other man. 'Evelyn told me I would find Eve up here,' he bit out tautly.

Adam's mouth twisted. 'Only because Eve hasn't yet found an opportunity to tell her grandmother the wedding is off.'

Paul's head went back challengingly. 'As far as I'm concerned, it isn't!'

'Fortunately, what you think doesn't come into it,' Adam returned hardily.

Eve gave a pained wince as he deliberately taunted the other man, knowing she was the cause of this awful scene. But Adam had been so understanding with her earlier concerning the decision she had been forced to make; unfortunately, his dislike of Paul prevented him according the other man the same dignity. It didn't really help that she knew the reaction would probably have been even worse if the roles had been reversed; they were *worse* than schoolboys.

And poor Adam's jaw was already beginning to show signs of discoloration.

She frowned at him worriedly. 'I think you should go and get a cold compress for that to try and keep the swelling down.'

He glanced at the other man with narrowed eyes. 'It can wait,' he decided dismissively.

'Don't delay on our account,' Paul taunted hardily.

'I wouldn't think of leaving just yet,' Adam returned mockingly.

'Will you two just stop this?' Eve put up a hand to her throbbing temple, the strain of the day beginning to tell on her. The last thing she felt in the mood for was being emotionally dragged about by these two men like a rag doll!

Adam's expression instantly became one of concern, and he moved protectively towards her.

Eve stepped back instinctively as she saw the anger snapping in Paul's eyes.

The movement had been pure force of habit, but nevertheless she didn't want a repeat of the violent outburst of a few minutes ago.

'Adam, I really think it might be better if you went downstairs and got something for that bruising,' she told him firmly.

His mouth tightened, and he looked from Paul's triumphant face to her wearily resigned one before nodding reluctant acquiescence.

But, being Adam Gardener, he couldn't just leave. Oh, no, that would have been too easy!

'Don't let him get to you,' he murmured, before bending his head to lightly brush his lips against hers.

Eve glanced over his shoulder at Paul's furious face, knowing that, however much Adam might have enjoyed the kiss, he hadn't done it for that reason. 'Swine,' she muttered, for Adam's ears alone.

He was grinning as he stepped back. 'Just call if you need me,' he said, provocatively loud enough for the other man to hear.

Paul was still scowling when the two of them had been left alone up in the studio. 'What was that supposed to mean?' he ground out.

She shook her head impatiently. 'Adam was deliberately trying to goad you.' And he had more than succeeded, she conceded wearily. Would today *never* come to an end?

Paul thrust his hands into his trouser pockets, a pair of the expensively tailored variety that he always wore, a navy blue pair this afternoon, with a sports jacket bearing a grey and navy blue check. Paul always looked perfectly tailored, no matter what the occasion.

'I resent the fact,' he bit out, 'that a man like Adam Gardener believes he has the right to do that. How could you, Eve?' He looked pained. 'How could you come straight from shattering all my hopes and plans into Adam Gardener's arms?'

Not literally, of course; a few hours had elapsed since she saw Paul at his flat, but it was close enough to make her feel heavy with guilt. How *could* she have done that? If she knew the answer to that, there would probably never have been the need to cancel her plans to marry Paul. It was not knowing how she felt about Adam that confused her so much.

But an answer like that wouldn't satisfy Paul, as it hasn't earlier. And why should it? The two of them had given almost a year of their lives in commitment to each other, and yet within a few days of her meeting Adam it had all been destroyed. She acknowledged that she owed Paul more than that, and yet she couldn't think of any other answer than releasing him from his unspoken promises to her. And releasing herself from her unspoken promises to him. Because she could no longer keep them.

Paul looked haggard, a white line of tension about his mouth. 'I came here to tell you I still love you, that this—madness, with Adam Gardener, changes nothing for me.'

And he had found her in the other man's arms! 'I'm so sorry,' she choked.

'I'm not giving up, Eve,' he told her evenly. 'Adam Gardener was wrong a few minutes ago; *we're* the ones who were made for each other.'

Eve blushed at the thought of Paul overhearing that conversation, of the things Adam had said next. It must have seemed to Paul as if at any moment she and Adam were about to go to bed together. And, despite her attraction to Adam, she liked to believe they wouldn't have done.

'Just think, Eve,' Paul persuaded lightly, 'We come from the same background, have the same friends, the same interests, want the same things out of life.'

Except when it came to her career and anything connected to it.

Strange, how even since this morning she had realised the fundamental differences they had when it came to that. And, important as Paul was to her life, her painting was important to her too, not in competition with him as he almost seemed to regard it, but as a way of enriching their lives through her own sense of self-achievement.

'You're thinking of all this, aren't you?' Paul made a sweeping movement with his arm around the room as he seemed to read her thoughts. 'Maybe I have been wrong in the way I've handled your career, but it's true that we learn from our mistakes. Eve, if you want publicity, then you'll have publicity. If you want to travel, then we'll do that too. I'm not in that much of a hurry to enter politics, I can take a few months off——'

'It's too soon for any of this, Paul,' she stopped him before he went any further, overwhelmed by his sudden change of heart. Not because she wanted any of what he was offering, but because he had always been so adamantly opposed to it before. His change of mind made her feel slightly off balance.

'But I love you,' he ground out.

She knew that he had to, otherwise he would never have come to her in this way after what she had said to him this morning. She knew he was a proud man, and that it must have taken a lot of effort on his part to come here at all.

And he had found her in Adam's arms.

She couldn't forget that fact, and felt mortified at the thought, hot all over at the memory.

But guilt and remorse couldn't make her do something that would probably ruin all their lives. She had to be more sure.

'And I love you,' she told him quietly. 'But, as you saw,' she gave herself no mercy, 'I feel something for Adam too.'

Paul's mouth tightened. 'If he wants a fight, he's going to get one!'

'I think you've already had one,' she reminded heavily.

'On the contrary,' Adam drawled as he walked back into the room, the ice-pack held against his jaw. 'I haven't even begun to fight,' he added tensely.

'You think you're so damned clever, don't you?' Paul rounded on him, his eyes glittering furiously. 'Eve may be fooled by you now, but she'll soon realise what you're really like when you walk out of her life, leaving it in tatters!'

Adam faced him coldly, his gaze steady. 'But I have no intention of walking out of Eve's life, either now or in the future.'

'But you'll do it anyway,' Paul scorned. 'Once you've taken what you want.'

Dark blond brows rose menacingly. 'And just what is it you think I "want" from her?' he queried mildly, only the pulse in his cheek telling of his anger.

Paul's mouth twisted, as yet unsuspecting of the other man's fury. 'Isn't it obvious?' he said disparagingly.

'Not to me.' Adam shrugged, still remaining deathly calm, although Eve could see he was becoming more coldly angry by the minute. 'You see,' he continued softly, nothing in his tone to betray the blow he was about to give, 'I want Eve to marry me.'

To say Paul looked stunned was an understatement; he looked shattered, as if Adam had lethally dealt him the vicious blow he had been prevented from giving him earlier. All the breath seemed to be knocked from Paul's body as he paled to a sickly grey colour.

Eve moved forward concernedly. 'Paul——'

He shook off her concern, his attention all on the other man. 'What did you say?' he managed to choke, still that awful grey colour.

'I said I want to marry Eve,' Adam repeated calmly, the ice-pack discarded on the table. 'And I resent the remarks you made implying that she could be seduced into a physical relationship with me.' His eyes were steely.

Paul ignored the threat in the other man's voice, turning to Eve now, groaning her name in questioning disbelief for what he had just been told.

'I haven't accepted him,' she hastily assured him; Adam hadn't exactly *made* a proposal yet, more stated it as a fact as he saw it. Which wasn't necessarily the same way everyone saw it!

'I should hope not,' Paul gasped, outraged at the thought. 'You've only known the man a few days, you know nothing about him!'

Thanks to Adam, the time before Paul arrived had been taken up with finding out more about him than some women perhaps learned in a lifetime with a man.

She felt she knew him *rather* well after that. And she could see by the mocking smile on Adam's lips that he thought so too.

'I've told you, Paul,' she spoke more sharply than she intended because she was so conscious of Adam's speculative gaze on them both, 'I just need time to think.' Without pressure from either of these two men, she might have added, but didn't, because she knew them both well enough to realise it would do no good; they were equally strong-willed in their individual ways!

'Well, I don't intend to be far away while you're doing it.' Paul's words were meant for Eve, but he continued to look challengingly at the other man.

'It goes without saying that I'll want to spend as much time with Eve as I possibly can.' Adam met the challenge—and more! 'After all, we have the New York exhibition to discuss in fine detail,' he added with deliberate provocation.

Paul's eyes narrowed to icy slits—as expected! 'What New York exhibition?' he grated.

'Oh, hasn't Eve told you about that?' Adam feigned surprise. 'In that case, just forget I ever mentioned it.'

She was going to scream at the two of them in a minute. Much, *much* worse than schoolchildren! And she hadn't mentioned the New York exhibition, because she had no intention of doing it.

Paul gave Adam a coldly dismissive glance before turning to Eve. 'I'll call you tomorrow and we can arrange a time for me to come over so that we can discuss the business details that are outstanding,' he told her softly, affectionately. 'In the meantime, darling, take care.' He moved to kiss her lightly on the lips. 'Gardener,' he rasped dismissively as he raised his head, preparing to leave.

'Lester,' Adam returned icily.

'I'll walk you to the door,' Eve offered quickly, moving to join Paul.

His eyes blazed briefly with triumph, although he quickly had the emotion under control. 'I'd like that,' he told her warmly.

She glanced briefly at Adam, but he made no effort to either join them or leave the studio, just stood and watched them go with an expressionless face.

She barely heard what Paul was saying to her on the way downstairs, absently returned the brief kiss he gave her at the door, the second time he had done so in the last few minutes, although Eve hadn't really registered the fact, but simply responded out of force of habit. Her thoughts were on Adam, on the fact that he was still up in her studio. And that the charcoal sketch she had done of him earlier lay exposed on the top of her pad, if he should care to look at it.

He was standing with the pad in his hands as she came back into the studio. 'This is very good,' he told her without looking up, instantly aware of her presence in the room as soon as she quietly entered. 'A little flattering, perhaps, but then you do create images that are more beautiful than life in all your paintings.' He put the pad down, looking up at her at last.

Her sketch of Adam was completely true to life, without even an ounce of poetic licence attached to it.

'I didn't like him kissing you,' he finally bit out.

'I know,' she acknowledged flatly.

He nodded abruptly, watching her with narrowed eyes. 'You were very quiet while he was here.'

She shrugged. 'You two seemed to be saying it all.'

His mouth twisted. 'We were acting like a couple of idiots.'

Eve raised her brows. 'As long as you realise that.'

He grimaced at her derision. 'Man's natural urge to protect what he considers his.'

'Except that I don't *belong* to either of you,' she reminded waspishly.

'Man's natural urge to protect what he hopes to be his?' he corrected hopefully.

She couldn't help smiling at his wistful expression. 'How's the chin?' she teased.

'Sore as hell,' he admitted ruefully. 'For an idiot, Lester packs quite a punch.'

'For an idiot, you take quite a punch,' she returned pointedly. 'And did I forget to mention the fact that Paul used to be some sort of boxing champion when he was at university?'

'You little——' Adam broke off, chuckling softly. 'It seems,' he gave her a considering look, 'that there's a tigress on the loose—and *I* don't even have you by the tail yet! I'm beginning to wonder if there wasn't something in the way Lester kept you subdued and obedient, after all. Now, come on, Eve, you wouldn't strike an injured man?' He backed away as she began to advance purposefully towards him, mocking laughter glowing in the dark depths of his eyes. 'You would,' he decided, beating a hasty retreat. 'I think I'll just go and get a fresh ice-pack for my jaw!' He made no effort to touch her, realising he had already pushed his luck enough for one day.

Eve's smile faded as soon as she heard his footsteps going down the stairs.

He had only stated that he didn't like Paul kissing her and left it at that, but she had been all too aware of the furious glitter in his eyes. A repeat of the intimacy in front of him was likely to evoke a serious reaction, although Adam had done everything in his power after making the statement to dampen his anger and bring their conversation on to a lighter note.

And their bantering teasing had taken the edge off the confrontation with Paul. But that was all it had done, taken the edge off it, dulled the shock a little of knowing her love for Paul was no longer enough. Strange, she had always believed love between two people was enough to sustain a relationship. She just hadn't allowed for a man like Adam entering her life.

Now her life was no longer the planned and ordered thing she had always believed it to be, and she knew that she would have to go through even more soul-searching and pain before this whole sorry mess came to an end.

If it did.

But surely everything had to come to an end, one way or another.

Didn't it . . .?

CHAPTER EIGHT

'WHAT on earth is going on?' Marina wandered into the studio a few minutes later, beautiful as usual in a pale blue cotton top and matching thigh-length shorts. 'Paul arrived looking like a thundercloud, and left looking even blacker, and Adam—after spending most of the afternoon up here with you, I might add,' she pouted complainingly, 'is in the kitchen charming a second ice-pack out of Mrs Hodges. What on earth *happened* to his chin?' she probed, her eyes widely curious. 'You didn't hit him, did you?' She gasped as the idea suddenly occurred to her.

'Of course not,' Eve dismissed scathingly, the question really requiring no answer.

'Well, it certainly wasn't Paul, so——' She broke off speculatively as Eve's cheeks blushed hotly. 'Good heavens, he didn't?' she breathed disbelievingly, coming to sit on the edge of the table that stood next to Eve's easel and canvas, with little regard for her expensive clothing. 'What did Adam do to cause that reaction?' she prompted eagerly.

'I didn't say Paul had hit him...'

'You didn't have to,' Marina scorned. 'Good lord, I still can't believe it of old Paul,' she said in amusement, shaking her head.

145

'None of this was Paul's fault,' Eve snapped defensively.

'Then whose fault was it?' her cousin pounced.

She realised, too late, that she had admitted more than she had wanted to. Marina, as she knew of old, wasn't going to stop pestering her now until she had the full story out of her.

She gave a heavy sigh, deciding to keep this as brief as possible. 'You may as well know that I've decided to put off my wedding to Paul for a while,' she revealed stiffly.

Marina's eyes widened. 'You mean you've jilted him?' she gasped disbelievingly.

Eve's cheeks were flushed. 'I didn't say that.'

'Yes, you did,' her cousin dismissed scathingly. 'Goodness, he must still be wondering what's hit him!' she said with obvious relish.

Eve gave her a reproving look. 'Paul is naturally upset that I——'

'Upset?' Marina echoed scornfully, her brows raised incredulously. 'I should think the poor man is gnashing his teeth down to the gums!'

She frowned. 'It isn't going to be an easy time for any of us——' She broke off as Marina's gaze once again became speculative. 'I'm just a little uncertain about getting married at the moment, that's all,' she insisted. 'I still love Paul——'

'Just not enough to marry him,' Marina mused, her leg swinging casually back and forth.

'Marina,' she began warningly at her cousin's obvious enjoyment of the situation.

'OK.' She held up her hands submissively. 'But I really would like to know what you and Adam were doing in here when Paul arrived, to make him actually resort to hitting Adam.'

She gave a heavy sigh at her cousin's persistence. 'I didn't say we were *doing* anything.'

'You mean Paul just walked in and jumped to the conclusion that you were?' Marina nodded with tongue-in-cheek understanding. 'Did you tell him before or after he hit Adam that the wedding was off?' she added innocently.

'Marina!' said Eve exasperatedly. 'The wedding has only been cancelled,' she insisted again firmly, 'until I feel more sure about things.'

'You've loved Paul since the year dot and you suddenly feel "unsure" of things?' Her cousin shook her head incredulously. 'I think my idea of marrying for money has a lot to be said for it, after all!'

'It's cynical and—and underhand,' Eve rebuked frowningly.

Marina shrugged. 'It's only underhand if the other person doesn't know about it.'

'You mean the poor man would know you were only after his money?' She gasped at this unexpected honesty.

'And life-style.' Her cousin nodded, pouting thoughtfully. 'Anything else *would* be underhand.'

Marina's philosophy on life and love was completely foreign to her! 'Then why on earth should he marry you, knowing you only want his money—and life-style?' she pointed out practically.

Her cousin stood up, grinning. 'Because all that money will ensure that I'm completely faithful, and also suitably adoring. And besides,' she added saucily as she stood up, 'I have a great body!'

Eve was still shaking her head dazedly long after Marina had gone back downstairs. How could they, two women who had the same upbringing, have such different outlooks on life?

The fact that thousands of other woman had 'great bodies' didn't daunt Marina in the least; she was so confident of her own capabilities. And, knowing Marina as she did, Eve didn't doubt her cousin had the confidence to achieve exactly what she wanted to!

All of which didn't alter the turmoil in her own life one little bit. And she still had to break the news of the cancelled wedding to everyone else...

Sophy's reaction was so predictable, it almost went without saying. Almost.

'I think it's the best thing you've ever done,' she said once Eve had joined the other couple in the garden and she had told them the news. 'Maybe now we can get down to talking sensibly about an exhibition.'

'Darling, now isn't the time to be discussing that,' Patrick put in reprovingly. 'Eve needs time to adjust, to get over——'

'The wisest decision she ever made?' his wife scorned. 'Anyone with any sense—or who isn't in love with the man—can see him for exactly what he——'

'Sophy, I said leave discussing the exhibition until another time.' Again Patrick interrupted, his tone measured, but none the less effective for all that. 'We have some packing to do, I believe, Sophy,' he added pointedly.

'But——'

'Take care of yourself, Eve.' Patrick ignored Sophy's protest, bending down to kiss Eve warmly on the cheek. 'And if you need someone to talk to, give me a call,' he encouraged softly.

'Yes, do call us,' Sophy added distractedly, giving her a light hug.

'I said *me*, Sophy,' Patrick corrected drily. 'You can hardly be called a sympathetic ear!'

She drew in an angry breath. 'I——'

'Good news, everyone.' Marina strolled out of the house, closely followed by Adam. 'I've persuaded Adam to stay on here instead of going back to London to an impersonal hotel.'

Eve looked at her sharply, not fooled for a minute by the guilelessly innocent expression in those wide blue eyes. Marina knew exactly what she was doing, and was relishing her role as matchmaker.

Her cousin could be so unpredictable: until this afternoon she had been flirting with Adam for all she was worth; now that she knew there was something—although she wasn't quite sure what it was—

between Adam and Eve, she was throwing the two of them together as if she had never shown the slightest interest in him herself. It was this very unpredictability that made her such an enigma at times.

Eve's attention turned to Adam, looking for some sign of triumph within him. Once again it wasn't there, only an air of satisfaction—that things were working out so well in his favour.

'How nice,' she responded non-committally.

'You know, Marina,' Sophy drawled slowly, her eyes narrowed to jade slits, 'maybe I've underestimated you all these years; we have more in common than I'd realised.' She put her arm through the crook of Marina's as they turned back towards the house. 'Perhaps we could arrange to have lunch together when we get back to town?' she suggested brightly.

'Perhaps we could,' Marina responded mischievously as they entered the house.

'I have some packing to do,' Patrick excused hastily, as he suddenly felt in the way.

Eve was aware of Adam watching her closely, but she deliberately kept her face expressionless, not really sure yet how she felt about the fact that he wouldn't be leaving today after all.

One thing she did know, these feelings of manipulation were really beginning to grate on her!

'Marina made the invitation,' Adam told her softly once the others had left, moving to stand close beside her. 'And as I really do have this aversion to the impersonality of hotels . . .'

Eve gave him a sceptical glance before turning to look out over the garden where her grandmother was tending her roses in complete innocence of the machinations that were taking place around her eldest granddaughter to confuse and befuddle her life.

Her grandmother had disappeared among her precious blooms almost immediately after Eve had announced the cancellation of her wedding to Paul, as if she had difficulty coming to terms with the news. They would have a long chat together later.

'Is it so wrong of me to want to spend more time with you?' Adam prompted huskily at her silence.

'A little unfair, don't you think?' she answered without turning.

'Is it fair that I can't touch you and love you as I want to?' he ground out fiercely. 'Is it fair that I have to stand by and watch everyone bathed in your warmth but me? Is it fair that I tremble like a young boy when I stand close to you like this? Is any of *that* fair, Eve? Is it?'

She knew he wasn't responsible for what was happening between them, but was as much a victim of this lightning desire as she was.

'I'm sorry.' Her smile was tentative as she turned to him. 'Of course you're a very welcome guest here.'

'Am I?' His dark gaze searched her face. 'Am I really?'

'Yes.' Her reply was breathless, her own gaze caught up in those chocolate-brown depths. 'I— you didn't finish telling me your life story earlier,' she prompted briskly to escape his spell.

He shrugged. 'When I left college I borrowed some money from my father and played about with stocks and shares. I was one of the lucky ones, I was successful at it.'

She had the feeling he would be successful at whatever he set out to do. That was what worried her!

'I paid my father back his money from my profits,' Adam continued dismissively. 'And after that I began to invest directly into businesses I thought showed potential—and a reasonable profit for me! Once I'd mastered that, I decided to go into the ownership business myself. End of story.'

She knew that wasn't the end at all, that the years since he had left college had been hard and sometimes difficult; the mark of those years was in the hardness of his face and the cool, enigmatic mask he sometimes wore. But he obviously wasn't in a mood to discuss that.

'I own and live in an apartment in Manhattan,' he continued softly. 'But I can run my business organisation from anywhere in the world I choose.' Even here, in this house, he seemed to say without actually voicing the words.

'You obviously enjoy the challenge of what you do.' Eve chose to ignore the unspoken statement.

'It has its excitements,' he conceded with a casual shrug.

'We live very quietly here,' she told him abruptly.

'I'm sure I'll survive,' he drawled at her effort to put him off staying here.

She moved her shoulders dismissively. 'I hope you won't be too bored.'

'Excitement can take many forms, Eve,' he said softly, his gaze holding hers. 'I haven't been bored for a single moment in your company so far. And I don't expect that to change. When will you realise that I'm not some callow youth who doesn't know what he really wants out of life?' He sounded irritated.

She didn't for a moment doubt his maturity—or his determination!

'As for staying here,' Adam looked around them appreciatively, 'it could be our own paradise,' he told her mischievously, grinning as she gave a pained frown at the pun. 'Do you think your grandmother will let us rename the house Garden of Eden after we're married? I know,' he held up silencing hands as she went to make a cutting reply, 'you don't believe that will ever happen. But if you take away a man's dreams, Eve,' he sobered, 'you take away his reason for living.'

What about a woman's dreams? She had dreamt of marrying Paul for the majority of her life, and now that dream had come within her reach she had chosen not to take it.

Maybe you should never try to make dreams fit into reality.

'I don't understand the young people of today.' Her grandmother shook her head with feeling. 'Marina has invited Adam to stay on here, which is perfectly all right with me; he's such a nice young man. But now Marina tells me that she intends leaving tonight herself!' she said exasperatedly.

This was news to Eve, although she couldn't say she was altogether surprised. Sophy and Marina seemed to have put their heads together over this—despite Patrick's protestations, Eve felt sure—and come up with the idea of leaving Eve and Adam to their own devices.

'How can Marina think of just going off like that and leaving her own guest?' their grandmother still frowned. 'Oh, never mind that for now,' she dismissed with impatience. 'I'm sure Marina has her reasons.' Although she obviously had no idea what they could be! 'Tell me, how are you, darling?' she prompted concernedly.

It was the first opportunity the two of them had had to talk privately, Sophy and Patrick leaving after tea, Marina staying for dinner before she too left. Adam had discreetly disappeared at the same time as Marina had gone upstairs to do her packing, leaving Eve and her grandmother alone in the lounge.

How was she? She wasn't really sure. Yesterday she had been going to marry Paul, today she felt as if she were adrift in a tumultuous ocean. Her life was suddenly all loose ends with nothing to tie on to. And it made her feel very vulnerable.

'As you can imagine,' she sighed, 'Paul isn't very pleased——'

'I didn't ask how Paul was,' her grandmother cut in firmly. 'I want to know how you are.'

'Feeling exposed. Vulnerable,' she admitted. 'Weak,' she added tautly.

Her grandmother gave her a puzzled look. 'Weak?' she repeated gently. 'I think what you've done is very brave. A lot of women would have felt compelled to go on with the wedding at this late stage, no matter what their feelings of uncertainty. Divorce may be easy nowadays if the marriage doesn't work out, after all, but I've always believed that prevention is so much easier than cure. So you mustn't feel in the least weak, darling.' She patted Eve's hand reassuringly.

Much as she loved her grandmother, Eve didn't feel she could explain to her just yet that the weakness she was experiencing was an attraction to a man other than Paul. If it had all seemed to happen so suddenly to her, how much more confusing her grandmother would find it all!

'It will work out, darling,' she told Eve with certainty. 'In whatever way is for the best, I'm sure.'

Eve only wished *she* knew what was for the best! Like many people before her, she wished she were able to see into the future and know that things had worked out for them all. If that were possible!

'Would you like to talk about it?' her grand-mother suggested seeing the uncertainty in her eyes.

'Not yet.' She gave a rueful grimace. 'It's all still such a nightmare.'

'Whenever you feel ready.' She squeezed Eve's hand understandingly. 'Now,' she added briskly, 'you can help me with the problem of what we're to do with Adam while Marina disappears back to London!'

'My grandmother isn't quite sure what to do with you,' Eve murmured softly against Adam's chest, enveloped by his masculine warmth.

He chuckled softly, the sound vibrating against her ear as he played with silky tendrils of her hair. 'Tell Evelyn she doesn't need to worry about it, you can take very good care of me.'

Eve grimaced, shaking her head. 'I think she's confused enough already, without that.'

He shrugged beneath her, lightly kissing her brow. 'She likes me; that should make it easier.'

There could be no doubting the fact that her grandmother liked him. But then, hadn't Eve known the first time she looked at him that Adam would find favour in her grandmother's eyes? Eve's own grandfather had been a similar type of man, tall and handsome, and as strong inside as he looked on the outside; and her grandmother had been married to him for thirty happy years before his unexpected death. Adam and her grandmother were like kindred spirits!

'This shouldn't be happening.' Eve turned her face into Adam's chest with a groan.

'When it comes to love, the words "shouldn't", "couldn't" and "wouldn't" cease to exist,' he murmured softly against the creaminess of her cheek.

She couldn't think straight with him touching her like this, her heart racing, her breath coming in ragged gasps. 'But that can't happen between us,' she protested feebly.

'"Can't" is just another way of saying "couldn't",' he dismissed harshly.

'Adam, listen to me,' she pleaded, trying to stop the destructive path of those marauding lips down her throat to the sensitive hollows of its base, hollows that Adam had already discovered were highly sensitive to his slightest touch.

She looked down at his face, which was slightly flushed with passion; the blush that came to her own cheeks was for quite another reason—as she knew the rakish disorder of his hair was due to her caressing fingers at the height of their passion.

'I'm not like this,' she groaned. 'This isn't me!'

'Of course it's you,' he reproved gently. 'The woman you become in my arms.'

She had lost track completely of how long she had been in his arms, had shut herself away in her studio earlier in the hope that she could lose herself in her work, only to have Adam come up to join her. She hadn't been able to resist when he'd taken her in his arms, laid her down on the sofa and joined her there, his mouth and hands knowing her intimately.

Once again she had known the aching dismay of not being able to say 'no' to him, and once again Adam had been the one to be strong for both of them, assuring her that they had time, that there was no rush. He had been the one to soothe and calm her until desire throbbed only dully, holding her in his arms as she had begun to talk of her grandmother's confusion.

Could this really be her, as he said, the real her, this vibrantly alive woman who only seemed to exist for the times she could be in Adam's arms like this?

It didn't seem possible this other woman, a woman she didn't really know, could have been inside her all the time. Why couldn't she have come alive like this in Paul's arms?

'Sweetheart, don't dwell on what should have been but wasn't,' Adam urged softly as he read the pain in her eyes. 'Just think about the two of us, here, together, now.'

'But——'

'Let's talk about the arrangements for Christmas,' he put in lightly.

'Christmas?' She gasped; if he had been hoping to disconcert her, he had succeeded! 'But you just said we should only think of now.'

'And us, here, together,' he reminded with a soft reproving tap on the end of her nose. 'And things like where to spend Christmas can be the cause of friction between a lot of couples.'

Eve sat up abruptly. 'We aren't a couple. And Christmas is months away yet!'

'I may be a thirty-eight-year-old liberated man,' Adam continued as if she hadn't made the protest, 'but when it comes to Christmas I'm pretty old-fashioned; I always spend the festive season with my folks in New York. But I'm sure that this year, as you always have Christmas here with your family, it would be easier if my parents just flew over and stayed here for a few days. They're really looking forward to meeting you, by the way,' he added teasingly.

'You can't have told them about me!' she groaned disbelievingly.

'The day after I first met you.' He nodded. 'I told them then that you were very special. And when I realised you were The Unicorn I just couldn't wait to share that news with them too. I had your grandmother's permission to call them while the two of you talked earlier. My parents couldn't have been more thrilled for me. They knew that I've always had a special love for your work, so it was only natural I would love you too. Last year I gave my parents one of your paintings for Christmas; this year I'll be able to give them the real thing!'

Eve looked uncertain. How could he remain so one-hundred-per-cent sure, when she didn't know what *she* was feeling from one moment to the next?

'A little faith—and not *too* much time, I hope—and things will work out, you'll see,' he assured her softly. 'I don't really think——'

'I thought I might find the two of you up here,' drawled a lightly mocking voice.

Eve pulled abruptly out of Adam's arms, her expression one of guilt as she looked across the room at Marina; the other woman had come upon them so quietly that neither of them had been aware of her presence, Eve felt sure. Although, typically, Adam didn't look in the least disconcerted by the interruption, or the intimacy in which they had been found!

She shot him a reproving look as he merely grinned a greeting to Marina.

'Stop acting so coy, Eve,' her cousin derided impatiently. 'If you want my opinion, dumping Paul and falling in love with Adam are the two most sensible things you've ever done in your life; and we both know how practical you've always been!'

Bright spots of angry colour burnt Eve's cheeks. 'I haven't *dumped* Paul, and I'm not in love with Adam.'

'Then maybe you should have been the one to go into acting,' Marina told her dismissively, turning to Adam, completely ignoring Eve's angry gasp at the taunt. 'I thought at the time that Eve was lucky to be sharing a bathroom with you,' she teased wryly.

'I know perfectly well what you're implying,' Eve snapped. 'But Adam has behaved the perfect gentleman as far as those communicating doors are concerned!'

Marina's eyes narrowed as she continued to look at Adam. 'It's serious, then?'

'No!'

'Yes.'

Eve and Adam answered together, Eve heatedly, Adam with total calmness—and conviction.

'I hoped it was.' Her cousin nodded. 'In that case, could I see you for a few minutes before I leave, Adam?' Marina's flamboyance had left her now, her manner was almost tentative, an emotion completely out of character.

Adam sobered instantly, also alerted by something in her manner. 'Of course.' He nodded.

Marina glanced uncomfortably at Eve. 'Alone,' she added abruptly.

Eve frowned her puzzlement; earlier Marina had seemed determined to throw Adam and herself together; could it now be that her cousin regretted her impetuosity?

What other reason could she have for asking to be alone with Adam now?

Whatever Marina's reasons, Eve had no choice but to excuse herself. 'I'll just go down and say goodnight to Grandmother.'

'Eve,' Adam halted her at the door, and she turned slightly, not quite able to look at him. 'Don't forget to come back,' he said softly.

Come back to what, though? she puzzled as she went down the stairs.

What was Marina up to?

CHAPTER NINE

WELL, she certainly wasn't going to get the answer to that from Adam, for he excused himself directly after breakfast the next morning, claiming he had a business meeting in London.

The fact that he would be out for the day didn't particularly worry Eve; after all, she had work to do herself this morning at the library, and this afternoon would be taken up with her painting. It was the fact that Adam hadn't previously mentioned the business meeting that bothered her, and she had a strange feeling that his conversation last night with Marina was all mixed up in it. He had been grim-faced the evening before when she'd returned to the studio after talking to her grandmother, shrugging off her concern with his usual teasing manner, although for once she had the feeling the lightness was forced.

And now, this morning, he was disappearing to London for the day.

Her grandmother shook her head as she watched Adam's long, easy strides of departure. 'He's the strangest house-guest I've ever known. What do you suppose is going on between him and Marina?' She frowned her puzzlement.

Eve wished she knew!

She was very preoccupied at the library that morning, and her mood wasn't helped by Paul telephoning to say he thought that afternoon would be a good time for them to discuss business. It wasn't a good time for her, it was the last thing she felt like doing today, but she realised that Paul was a busy man and that it was only through someone cancelling an appointment that he was able to see her that afternoon. Besides, a drive into town might help to clear her head a little, she tried to convince herself.

But it became apparent after only a few minutes that Paul had little or no interest in discussing business himself, that he was still very involved with the problem of Adam in their lives. Wasn't everybody?

'I'm having someone check into his past, Eve,' Paul told her grimly. 'I want to know exactly——'

'You've done what?' She gasped disbelievingly, her head suddenly very clear.

His eyes flashed angrily. 'Don't sound so surprised, Eve,' he dismissed hardily. 'I realised yesterday, when I told you that you don't really know the man, just how true that is. I'm interested to know how he acquired his wealth, how——'

'Through sheer hard work!' She stood up to agitatedly pace the room, all the time looking at Paul as if she had never seen him before as he sat so calmly behind his imposing desk. As, indeed, she was beginning to doubt. 'You can't be serious about this.' She shook her head incredulously.

'Of course I'm serious,' he said impatiently. 'Eve, be sensible about this,' he sighed as she still looked stunned by what he was doing. 'He could have any number of skeletons in his closet.'

And Paul was determined to flush them all out. It was unbelievable.

Her mouth was tight. 'I wish you had talked this over with me before going ahead with it.'

'You're infatuated with the man, you were sure to have said "no",' Paul dismissed scathingly.

'I would have said "no" because it's an invasion of his privacy!' she returned heatedly.

He shook his head sadly. 'I can't bear to see you making a fool of yourself over this man.'

'I'm not.' She controlled herself with effort, realising she was starting to sound slightly hysterical. But what Paul had done was—well, it was—well, she was at a loss for words! 'I want you to know here and now that I completely disapprove of what you're doing,' she bit out stiltedly. 'And that no matter what you find out about Adam, I don't want to know about it. I prefer to make up my own mind about people,' she added with distaste for his method.

'I was hoping to have had some initial information back by the time you got here this afternoon.' Paul frowned, seeming not to realise how angry his delving into Adam's private life had made her.

'I mean it, Paul. I'm not interested in what dirt you manage to dig up,' she snapped coldly. 'Now, if you don't mind,' she picked up her bag, 'I'd like to leave.'

'But, Eve——'

'I'm certainly not in the mood now to discuss business,' she cut in warningly.

Something in her tone finally got through to him, and he stood up to come around his desk to her, putting his hands lightly on her shoulders as he gazed down at her. 'Darling, I'm sorry if all this has upset you, but I don't——'

'Upset me?' she echoed tautly. 'You've *shocked* me! Your behaviour is like something out of an old black and white movie! No one looks into another person's life for dirt in real life.'

He flushed his displeasure at her criticism. 'Of course they do, Eve.'

'Not in my world, they don't,' she stated firmly, shrugging off his hands. 'Now, you can go ahead with this ridiculous business if you want to, but leave me out of it. And certainly don't even attempt to tell me anything of what you find out,' she repeated with distaste.

'Eve, listen to me——'

'If it's more of the same nonsense, then I don't want to hear it,' she warned him harshly.

He sighed. 'All right, I won't talk about that any more—for now. But when I do find out something underhand about him, I don't intend——'

'*If* you do,' she corrected stiffly, her eyes flashing deeply turquoise.

She was sure that if there had been anything like that in Adam's past, then he would have told her about it last night; he had gone into pretty graphic detail about everything else in his life! Certainly, nothing in his manner had given her the impression he was holding anything back from her.

'When I do,' Paul insisted harshly, his gaze narrowed on her with slight contempt for what he believed to be her gullibility. 'You really are infatuated with the man, aren't you?'

No, she realised sadly, she didn't believe she was infatuated with Adam at all; in just a few short days she had come to love him. And that knowledge hadn't helped to solve her dilemma at all. Now she was just aware of loving two men at the same time!

She had no idea how she had come to fall in love with Adam so quickly, or at all; she had just known last night that it was a fact. Marina had said she was in love with him, and, even as she had been indignantly denying it, she had known like a lightning bolt that it was the truth. If she had needed any further proof of it, she had got it when the jealousy ripped through her at Marina's request to be left alone with Adam.

But, as she was very much aware, loving Adam just made the situation even more complicated.

'I just disapprove of you probing into Adam's private life.' She evaded having to answer the accusation. 'And as I don't believe either of us is in the mood to discuss business...' She prepared to leave.

'Let's go out and have afternoon tea somewhere,' Paul suggested impulsively, the subject of his investigation into Adam forgotten—for now, as he had said. He squeezed her hands affectionately. 'Like we used to,' he encouraged huskily.

Reminding her of how things 'used to' be made Eve feel guilty rather than nostalgic. He really didn't deserve to have this happen to him.

'That would be nice,' she accepted softly, but without any real enthusiasm for the idea.

She knew the choice of restaurant had been deliberate—it was one of the places they had visited regularly together during happier times—but she deliberately kept the conversation as impersonal as possible. Which wasn't all that easy when Paul seemed determined to do the opposite!

She was feeling rather ragged by the time she drove back to Ashton House, her mood not improved when she learnt Adam hadn't returned yet.

He didn't get back in time for dinner either, although her grandmother did say she had received a telephone call from him to make his excuses and to explain he would be back later that evening. Like her grandmother, Eve was coming to think of him as the *strangest* house-guest!

She was too restless to work, too eaten up with curiosity as to Adam's whereabouts to relax. So much for 'seeing as much of her as he possibly could', she thought ruefully as she wandered outside in the late evening light. What *was* the man doing all this time?

'That face is far too beautiful to wear a frown.'

She spun around joyfully at the sound of his voice, all her disappointment and frustration at his absence completely disappearing as he stood so suddenly before her, launching herself against him eagerly, too pleased to see him to think of holding back or hiding her pleasure at seeing him.

'Mm,' Adam murmured appreciatively when he at last raised his head slightly, his lips only fractionally above her. 'If I'd known I was going to get this sort of reception, I would have come back sooner!'

Her eyes were glowing like jewels after the kiss they had just shared, her body moulded against the lean length of his. 'Why didn't you?' she gently rebuked, her voice husky.

A shadow darkened his face, the humour fading from his eyes. 'I had some important business to take care of, and it took longer than I'd realised.'

Eve looked up at him searchingly. 'It was very sudden, wasn't it?'

'No, I—— Yes, it was,' he amended heavily, moving away to hold her at arm's length. 'Eve, we have to talk,' he told her intently.

She sighed. 'Not tonight, surely? Paul has been talking all afternoon, and——'

'Lester was here?' Adam prompted sharply, and Eve could feel how tense he had become by the increased pressure of his hands on her shoulders.

'No, I went to see him,' she explained with a puzzled frown. 'That business we had to discuss,' she reminded, as Adam suddenly looked bleak.

The tension about his mouth relaxed a little, but not much. 'For a minute there, I—— But you would hardly have been so pleased to see me if you had decided to work things out with Lester,' he realised with relief. 'What business did the two of you have to discuss?' His eyes were narrowed.

'Adam!' She was taken aback at his probing; she knew she had shown she had been pleased to see him, but she had certainly never asked for the details of his own business dealings. However, she had the feeling he would have told her if she had shown the slightest curiosity!

'Just tell me whether or not you signed anything—anything new, that is,' he prompted impatiently.

'As it happens, we didn't actually get around to talking business,' she told him frowningly. 'Adam, what on earth is going on?' His attitude was beginning to alarm her.

'That's what I have to talk to you about,' he sighed. 'I found out some things about Lester that I think you should know.'

'Not you, too!' she denied incredulously.

Adam frowned. 'You mean you already know about Lester?'

'No—and I don't *want* to know, either!' she said exasperatedly. 'I'll tell you exactly the same thing I told Paul earlier, when he told me *he* was having *you* investigated; I consider it a complete invasion of privacy, and I have no wish to know what either of you found out about the other.' She glared at him, hurt that he could think he could sway her favour in his direction by finding out something disreputable about Paul; she just wasn't that shallow.

'So Lester is having me investigated,' he mused derisively. 'I wish him luck with it,' he mocked. 'I haven't been an angel, but I haven't been a devil either.'

'I just told you, I don't care what Paul finds out; I'm not interested!' Eve reminded stiltedly.

'Paul didn't find that out, I just told you,' Adam said softly, his eyes narrowed.

She turned away, still reeling from the blow of having him believe, as Paul did, that she could be so fickle as to change her feelings towards either of them because of something that had happened in their past.

'Eve, what I found out——'

'I told you,' she snapped, her eyes flashing, 'I don't want to know.'

He gave a heavy sigh of acknowledgement of her anger. 'What I found out doesn't concern Lester's past,' he continued reluctantly but remorsefully, 'but *your* future.'

'I don't want to know!'

'Eve, you aren't an ostrich, you can't bury your head in the sand,' he reasoned impatiently. 'And this is something you have to know about.'

'In your opinion,' she bit out tautly.

He shrugged. 'Are you interested in learning whether or not this house is still yours?' he asked hardily.

Her anger left her as suddenly as it had arrived, and she looked at him frowningly. 'What on earth are you talking about?'

'This house, and all the money you've made from your paintings——'

'Adam, you aren't making sense,' she cut in nervously.

'I found it necessary to go and see Lester. I had a few things I needed to talk to him about,' he added grimly, his eyes narrowed. 'He's downstairs now, with your grandmother and Marina; I think we should go and join them.'

'Paul and Marina are here?' she repeated dazedly—but she didn't fight it when Adam took hold of her arm and guided her down the stairs.

Her grandmother looked puzzled as she sat in one of the armchairs in the sitting-room, Marina stood tensely in front of one of the long windows that looked out over the garden—and whatever Adam had needed to discuss with Paul earlier it hadn't been of a verbal nature; if Adam's chin was still slightly discoloured from the other man's blow, then Paul himself was now sporting a cut lip and bruised cheek!

He glared at the other man, his expression sullen and uncooperative.

'Paul——'

'Don't waste your sympathy on him,' Adam rasped harshly. 'In the circumstances, he got let off lightly.'

'You surely didn't do this because you're in love with Eve?' Her grandmother frowned disbelievingly. 'I may be getting old, Eve,' she said impatiently as Eve turned to her in surprise, 'but there's nothing wrong with my eyesight!'

No, she acknowledged ruefully, her grandmother had known all the time of Adam's feelings for her, despite pretending she didn't. Just as she now knew of Eve's feelings for him, she realised with affectionate incredulity.

She had always thought her grandmother the wisest woman she had ever known, and once again she had proved it was so.

'The fact that I love Eve is all wrapped up in my actions of today, Evelyn,' Adam assured the older woman, turning with contempt towards Paul. 'This—this low-life——'

'Adam!' Eve gasped protestingly.

'He's being polite, in the circumstances,' Marina assured her hardily.

'What circumstances?' she said exasperatedly.

'I have a feeling Adam is about to tell us that, darling, if you will only let him,' her grandmother gently rebuked.

'Thanks, Evelyn.' Adam nodded, still looking grim. 'But I'm not about to do any explaining, Lester is.' He looked at the other man with dangerously narrowed eyes.

Paul shot him a resentful glare. 'The only person I have to talk to is Eve——'

'And her family,' Adam bit out tautly. 'They're involved too.'

'I don't accept that,' Paul told him condescendingly.

'Accept it,' rasped Adam abruptly, his stance one of aggression.

Paul gave a shaky sigh. 'Eve made me her business adviser with power of attorney.'

'Adviser is the relevant word in that statement,' the other man cut in harshly.

The bruise on Paul's cheek stood out lividly against his pallor. 'Eve is not business-minded——'

'And you think you are?' Adam derided scornfully.

Eve's feelings of nervousness had turned to panic as the conversation developed; there was a sick feeling in the pit of her stomach, and she was dreading, but already able to guess, what was coming next.

Paul's head was back challengingly. 'I have merely invested Eve's money for her.'

'In one get-rich-quick scheme after another—and they have all failed,' Adam cut in grimly. 'Would you like to tell Eve how much of her fortune she has left?'

Eve sat down on the chair behind her, her legs suddenly too weak to support her, her eyes like huge turquoise in her pale face as she stared up at a Paul who was beginning to seem like a stranger to her.

His mouth tightened. 'This latest venture I'm entering into with Dudley Graves should recoup——'

'It should, but it won't,' Adam bit out. 'You're a loser at business, Lester, can't you see that? You may want to be a big financier, but you don't have what it takes. And you don't have any of Eve's hard-earned cash left, either!'

She swallowed hard. 'None of it?'

'Eve, I've been investing for our future,' Paul turned to her pleadingly.

'None of it?' she repeated dully.

'A few thousand, that will be enough to recoup——'

'I thought you loved me,' she spoke over him as if she didn't hear him. 'I thought you were marrying me because you loved me——'

'Of course I am,' he told her dismissively, coming down on his haunches in front of her. 'Those losses are only a temporary setback, Eve,' he tried to take her hands in his, but she pulled back sharply. 'Dudley assures me that——'

'I don't care what Dudley assures you,' her voice rose shrilly, 'you had no right to use my money. No right!'

He straightened indignantly. 'As your lawyer, the man you were going to marry——'

'You should have taken her instructions, not used her money where you pleased without even discussing it with her,' Adam rasped.

Light blue eyes narrowed on him furiously. 'I've done nothing wrong.'

'Legally, no,' Eve's grandmother conceded harshly as she stood up to come to Eve's side, Eve still too numbed to respond, 'but morally you have done everything that is wrong.'

'Evelyn, you don't understand...'

'Don't talk to me as if I'm senile,' she snapped, the termagant of Eve's childhood back in full force. 'I understand perfectly. You're no better than a lying swindler; you took advantage of your privileged position as the family lawyer and Eve's affection for you. I never was completely sure of you when you took over from your father two years ago,' she murmured hardily. 'I never thought you were the man he was.'

'He was old-fashioned——'

'He was a gentleman!' Eve's grandmother stormed. 'A man to be trusted. Something you obviously are not. I don't believe there's any need, but I intend doing it anyway, to inform you that in future I will be taking my legal matters to a more trustworthy lawyer. And I believe you might find a few of your other clients doing the same when they hear how you conduct your affairs.' Her hand still rested comfortingly on Eve's shoulder, some of her strength passing down into her.

Paul looked furious at the statement. 'I'll have you in court on a libel charge.'

'For telling the truth?' she scorned, shaking her head. 'Whichever way a case like that went, your reputation would never recover.'

'Eve——'

'Don't touch me!' she warned stiffly, feeling as if she were about to break into a thousand pieces, would do so if the appealing hand Paul had reached out to her should make contact. 'Just tell me one thing,' she bit out shakily. 'Was it ever me you loved, or was it always the money and the prestige you thought it could give you?'

'Of course I loved you.'

'But having the money helped,' Marina scorned him.

Paul shot her a furious glare. 'What would you know about it—the daughter of a man who lost the family fortune in the first place?'

Marina's face paled to a ghostly white. 'I'm well aware of what my father did . . .'

'I've never heard such nonsense in all my life,' their grandmother cut in angrily. 'Your father was a wonderful businessman,' she assured Marina indignantly, 'and would have withdrawn from that particular deal if he had had the time. Unfortunately, I lost all my children before that could happen,' she added with emotion.

'You lost your money, too,' Paul derided contemptuously.

Blue eyes glittered furiously at him. 'I never, ever blamed my son for that.'

'Didn't you?' Marina looked at their grandmother hopefully. 'Didn't you really?'

'Of course not.' Evelyn sounded shocked at the idea. 'Your father made the family fortune in the first place by his astute investments. Surely you didn't think I in any way blamed him for what happened?' She frowned.

Marina shrugged. 'I heard two women gossiping about what had happened——'

'Gossip!' Their grandmother's tone told what she thought about that.

'It was at a garden fête you held here when I was fifteen,' Marina explained. 'These two women were saying what a shame it was your son had lost all the family money, what a pity it was the house had become so run-down.'

Those temper tantrums from Marina's teens were starting to be explained now, Eve realised: the constant need her cousin had to prove herself, to be the centre of attention always. And she could see their grandmother was beginning to see the same thing, too.

'None of that is true, darling,' she told Marina gently. 'We'll talk together later, and then I'll tell you what a wonderful man your father was.'

Marina's head went back in proud challenge as she turned once more to Paul. 'Whatever my father did he did by mistake, and not with deliberate intent as you did. I knew from the moment you tried to get me to go out with you a couple of years ago, because you thought I had come into money on my twenty-first birthday too, that you were no good,' she scorned. 'Oh, yes, you didn't always so heartily disapprove of me, did you?' she mocked with distaste as a ruddy hue coloured Paul's cheeks. 'A couple of years ago, before you took over from your father and were privy to our personal affairs, you would have been quite happy to settle for me and my legacy, if I had been interested—which I certainly wasn't. Good lord, even after you found out I hadn't received any money, you weren't averse to suggesting an affair between us might be fun!'

'Shut up,' Paul rasped, his jaw clenched. 'Just shut up.'

She shook her head. 'Eve's entitled to know the truth, all of it, now that I'm sure she no longer loves you. I've only kept quiet until now because she seemed to love you so much, and I thought perhaps ignorance was bliss,' Marina scorned.

'Eve still loves me,' Paul claimed angrily. 'She always has, she always will.'

What a fool she had been! So gullible, so ripe for the picking, so obviously in love with him. If it hadn't been for Adam and Marina—she hated to think what her life would have been like without the two of them!

'I wouldn't willingly breathe the same air you breathe now,' Eve told him coldly.

His mouth turned back. 'You always were a romantic little fool.'

Not any more, never any more.

'And you're a selfish swine,' Marina defended her like a lioness over one of her cubs. 'What a blow it must have been to your plans when you realised Eve had spent the majority of her money on restoring this house. Although even then I don't suppose all was completely lost; after all, the house might belong to my grandmother, but—forgive me, Grandmother,' she hugged her affectionately, 'Eve and I were sure to inherit it one day. And with the added knowledge now of Eve's earnings from her paintings, she must have seemed worth pursuing, after all.'

'I didn't need much pursuing,' Eve said self-disgustedly. 'I'd been in love with Paul, or thought I had, since I was a teenager!'

'In love with love, darling,' her grandmother put in gently. 'And that sort of love is usually the hardest to overcome. But as soon as you met Adam, your heart knew what it really wanted.'

'Another couple of months and it would have been too late,' Paul muttered angrily.

Another couple of months and she would have been married to this man, Eve realised with a shudder.

How blind she had been to what he was really like, while everyone around her could see him for exactly what he was!

Adam was watching her closely. 'Leave, Lester, while you're still able to do so,' he advised harshly.

Paul's mouth turned back contemptuously. 'So that you can take over my place in Eve's life?' he scorned. 'Maybe I'm a shark, Gardener, but you're a barracuda!'

'How unpleasant.' Eve's grandmother shuddered once he had swept arrogantly out of the room.

'But necessary,' Adam assured grimly.

'Oh, goodness, yes,' she agreed, giving him a warm smile. 'What a horrible young man he really is.'

More horrible and more devious than Eve could ever have imagined. She had trusted him with her power of attorney in good faith, had listened to his advice that it was the best thing to do. Naïveté, and believing herself in love with love—she could surely never have loved Paul if she had ever really known him!—had made her blind *and* stupid.

She didn't particularly care about the money, and, as Marina said, despite Adam's earlier misgivings, Ashton House belonged to their grandmother and couldn't be touched.

But it really was time she grew up.

CHAPTER TEN

'BEAUTIFUL. Just beautiful.'

'Perfectly lovely,' agreed another man.

'I'm glad we came,' said his companion.

Eve smiled at Sophy. 'Once again you've been proved right. The exhibition is a wonderful success.'

Sophy smiled mischievously. 'I have news for you, those two men aren't talking about your paintings, they're talking about you!' she confided with relish.

Eve spun around, and sure enough the two men in question weren't looking at any of the paintings on the walls, but at Eve herself.

Once she would have blushed at such openly appreciative stares, but the last five months she had attended so many interviews, been photographed from every angle possible, received such effusive flattery for both her work and herself, that she merely smiled at the two men, nodding acknowledgement of their compliments.

She took a glass of champagne off the silver tray as a waiter passed, sipping it appreciatively, Sophy following suit as she looked around the crowded gallery.

The exhibition in London had gone ahead amid a blaze of publicity concerning the revealed identity of The Unicorn. And while a certain amount of people, like the two admiring men across the room, had come here out of pure curiosity, the majority were seriously interested in her work and what it had to say.

'Is Adam coming tonight?' Sophy was watching her with narrowed eyes as she turned towards her.

'I've sent him an invitation.' She nodded, the calmness of her reply in no way revealing the aching loneliness of the last five months without him.

But it had been a loneliness of her own choosing. It would have been too easy, loving Adam as she did, to allow him to 'take over Paul's place in her life', as the other man had accused so scornfully, but she had needed the time alone, to grow, to learn about herself as a person without someone constantly there for her to lean on, to become emotionally independent for once in her life.

It had been a difficult thing to do, more difficult than she could ever have imagined, for it would have been so easy to turn to Adam for loving support. But five months later she knew the painful process of becoming completely independent had been worth it.

The question was, would Adam feel the same way about his own enforced loneliness?

When she had first told him what she intended to do, he had been adamant about not leaving her, especially when she had admitted to loving him; but she had finally persuaded him into believing she had to have this time, needed it desperately.

But five months without a single word of communication other than her invitation for tonight was a long time. Would he even bother to make an appearance? she wondered with inward concern.

She got her answer to that as he stood tall and handsome in the entrance to the gallery, his gaze moving slowly about the room until it came to rest on her. Eve felt her heart lurch with the gladness of seeing him again, but his expression revealed none of his emotions as he turned briefly to the couple who stood directly behind him, the elegantly beautiful woman, and arrogantly handsome man, instantly recognisable as his parents.

Eve turned to Sophy as she too watched Adam across the room. 'Sophy——'

'Leave them to me,' the other woman assured her firmly, putting down her own empty glass to pick up two full ones on her way to Adam's parents, pausing briefly in the middle of the gallery to greet Adam as he strode forcefully by.

Eve's hand tightening about the stem of her champagne glass was her only outward sign of tension.

Adam stopped mere inches in front of her, so dearly familiar in the black evening suit and snowy white shirt, his hair that glorious deep golden blond, his eyes dark and unfathomable.

'You're looking wonderful,' he finally said gruffly.

'So are you,' she returned softly, dismissing the beauty of the black and gold dress she had chosen with such care for just this meeting. 'You brought your parents with you.' She stated the obvious for something to say, suddenly shy with him.

'Yes,' he acknowledged, not even bothering to glance across the room in their direction, completely confident in Sophy's ability to take care of them. 'I thought it best if they came over with me.'

'Oh,' she answered non-committally.

'I got your invitation,' he told her, his eyes narrowed.

'Yes,' she agreed, the tension building between them.

Oh, God, let him still love her, she prayed. Because one thing the last months had shown her, she loved Adam more than anything else on earth, and wanted to spend the rest of her life with him if he would have her.

'A Christmas wedding might be nice, don't you think?' he remarked conversationally, just as if he were discussing the weather!

Eve felt the gladness in her heart, felt it burst and explode into bright, shattering light. It was going to be all right, after all. Adam still loved her and wanted her!

'I don't know if I can wait that long,' she admitted shakily, swaying towards him. 'I've missed you so much.'

His eyes glowed like warm honey. 'I didn't say we had to wait until then, only that it seemed a good time to get married. Oh, I love you, Eve,' he added with a groan.

'And I love you,' she replied with certainty.

He smiled warmly, his gaze holding hers as he reached in to his jacket pocket. 'Your invitation.' He handed her car keys back to her. 'And mine.' He held out his own car keys for her to take into her keeping.

They had to be the strangest exchange of love-gifts ever made, but Eve had sent him the car keys knowing he would understand their message, that he would realise she wasn't surrendering herself as a person, only her heart and soul into his keeping. As he had just entrusted himself to her.

'I can hardly wait to begin,' she accepted his invitation, holding the car keys as if they were more precious than any jewel, as indeed they were.

And there, in the midst of the crowded room, The Unicorn ceased to be elusive as she gave her love into Adam's keeping for all time, the two of them not caring that they had an audience as they moved into each other's arms, their lips meeting in eternal love.

THE IDEAL TONIC

Over the past year, we have listened carefully to readers
comments, and so, in August, Mills & Boon are launching
a *new look* Doctor-Nurse series – MEDICAL ROMANCES

There will still be three books every month from a wide
selection of your favourite authors. As a special bonus,
the three books in August will have a special offer price
of **ONLY** 99p each.

So don't miss out on this chance to get a real insight into
the fast-moving and varied world of modern medicine,
which gives such a unique background to drama, emotion
– and romance!

COMING SOON FROM MILLS & BOON!

Your chance to win the fabulous

VAUXHALL ASTRA
MERIT 1.2 5-DOOR

Plus

2000 RUNNER UP PRIZES OF WEEKEND
BREAKS & CLASSIC LOVE SONGS ON CASSETTE

♥ SEE
MILLS & BOON BOOKS ♥
THROUGHOUT JULY & AUGUST FOR DETAILS!

RUIT SALAD WORDSEARCH
COMPETITION!

ow would you like a years supply of Mills & Boon Romances ABSOLUTELY FREE? Well, you can win them! All you have to do is complete the word puzzle below and send it in to us by Dec. 31st. 1989. The first 5 correct entries picked out of the bag after that date will win **a years supply of Mills & Boon Romances** (*ten books every month - worth £162*) What could be easier?

T	E	T	A	N	A	R	G	E	M	O	P
A	N	E	Y	E	P	A	R	G	A	A	E
N	E	A	R	S	P	I	M	N	N	T	A
G	N	P	R	T	L	W	E	A	D	Y	C
E	I	R	E	R	E	I	L	R	A	R	H
R	R	I	B	A	U	K	O	O	R	R	M
I	A	C	P	W	R	C	N	O	I	E	A
N	T	O	S	B	A	R	K	E	N	H	N
E	C	T	A	E	E	F	R	C	U	C	A
I	E	T	R	R	P	O	G	N	A	M	N
T	N	A	R	R	U	C	D	E	R	L	A
E	E	H	C	Y	L	L	E	M	O	N	B

ASPBERRY   ORANGE   LYCHEE
EDCURRANT   MANGO   CHERRY
ANANA   LEMON   KIWI
ANGERINE   APRICOT   GRAPE
TRAWBERRY   PEACH   PEAR
OMEGRANATE MANDARIN   APPLE
LACKCURRANT NECTARINE   MELON

PLEASE TURN
OVER FOR
DETAILS
ON HOW
TO ENTER

HOW TO ENTER

All the words listed overleaf, below the word puzzle, are hidden in the grid. You can find them by reading the letters forward, backwards, up or down, or diagonally. When you find a word, circle it or put a line through it, the remaining letters (which you can read from left to right, from the top of the puzzle through to the bottom) will spell a secret message.

After you have filled in all the words, don't forget to fill in your name and address in the space provided and pop this page in an envelope (you don't need a stamp) and post it today. Hurry - competition ends December 31st. 1989.

Mills & Boon Competition,
FREEPOST,
P.O. Box 236,
Croydon,
Surrey. CR9 9EL

Only one entry per household

Secret Message _____

_____

Name _____

Address _____

_____

_____

_____ Postcode _____

You may be mailed as a result of entering this competition
Please tick the box if you are a Reader Service subscriber ☐

COMP7